"Oh, no. Not now."

"What—?" Max began to ask, but was cut off when the elevator jerked to a stop. Max reached out instinctively to steady Ryan when she stumbled. His hands lingered on her shoulders. "It stopped," he said unnecessarily, staring at the frozen floor numbers.

"It did this the other day," Ryan said with a sigh. "I was stuck in here for about ten minutes with—er—Santa Claus."

Max didn't smile. He pressed the alarm button, but nothing happened. Tugging at the collar of his shirt, he asked, "How long did you say you were stuck in here?"

"Ten minutes, roughly." She eyed him warily. "Don't tell me *you're* claustrophobic."

"Not usually. It's just that I don't relish being stuck in an elevator. What did you do?"

"Santa distracted me."

"A distraction, hmm? Sounds like a good idea," Max said. Then, before she had a chance to protest, he took her in his arms and lowered his lips to hers.

All I Want for Christmas

GINA WILKINS

HARLEQUIN®

TORONTO • NEW YORK • LONDON
AMSTERDAM • PARIS • SYDNEY • HAMBURG
STOCKHOLM • ATHENS • TOKYO • MILAN • MADRID
PRAGUE • WARSAW • BUDAPEST • AUCKLAND

ISBN-13: 978-0-373-19932-7
ISBN-10:   0-373-19932-5

ALL I WANT FOR CHRISTMAS

This is a work of fiction. Names, characters, places and incidents are either the product of the author's imagination or are used fictitiously, and any resemblance to actual persons, living or dead, business establishments, events or locales is entirely coincidental.

This edition published by arrangement with Harlequin Books S.A.

® and TM are trademarks of the publisher. Trademarks indicated with ® are registered in the United States Patent and Trademark Office, the Canadian Trade Marks Office and in other countries.

www.eHarlequin.com

Printed in U.S.A.

GINA WILKINS

A lifelong resident of Arkansas, romance bestselling author Gina Wilkins has written more than eighty books for Harlequin and Silhouette Books. She is a four-time recipient of the Maggie Award for Excellence presented by the Georgia Romance Writers, and she was a nominee for a Lifetime Achievement Award by *Romantic Times BOOKreviews*. She credits her successful career in romance to her long, happy marriage and three "extraordinary" offspring.

1

"PIP," six-year-old Kelsey whispered to her nine-year-old brother. "This mall is so crowded. How will we *ever* find our parents?"

It was the Friday after Thanksgiving, the busiest shopping day of the year. Drawn by well-advertised sales and a sudden, panicky awareness that Christmas was only a month away, shoppers had turned out in droves. And the mall was ready for them.

Cheery renditions of Christmas carols blared from unseen speakers. Dozens of artificial Christmas trees sparkled and glittered. Greenery, lights, tinsel and bows—it was a carefully choreographed Christmas wonderland.

Pip and Kelsey walked hand in hand through the chaos, wide-eyed and openmouthed. They were looking at a veritable wall of legs and backsides ahead of them.

"We'll find them," Pip said with a confidence that belied his nervous expression. "Don't worry."

Kelsey's faith in her older brother was unconditional and limitless. She smiled at him and squeezed his hand, trusting him to make everything right. Just as she'd always trusted him to take care of her.

A colorful gingerbread house had been constructed in the center of the lower level of the four-story mall. A front porch supported by large plastic peppermint canes held an inviting, oversize rocker. In it sat a plump figure dressed in red, whose warm smile gleamed from under a thick white beard. A long line of children waited to sit in his inviting lap, their eyes shining with anticipation and greed.

"Pip, look!" Kelsey pointed. "It's Santa."

Pip nodded, glancing from the gingerbread house to the dollar-a-ride train slowly circling in front of it. He was worried that Kelsey would want to ride the train; the ten dollars tucked into the pocket of his worn jeans wouldn't last long if they spent it on rides.

But Kelsey had another idea. "Let's get in line and talk to Santa. He'll know where we can find our parents."

Pip winced. "Kelsey..."

She was tugging at his hand, pulling him toward the end of the long, restless line of children. "He'll know, Pip," she said confidently, looking up at him with her enormous, bright blue eyes. "I'm sure he will."

Pip started to speak, but found he couldn't shake the unwavering trust in Kelsey's eyes. He shrugged. "Okay, you can talk to him. But don't expect too much, Kels. After all, he's just one of Santa's helpers, remember? And whatever you do, don't tell him we're here by ourselves, okay? He'll call the welfare people."

Kelsey's eyes grew even rounder. She shook her head vigorously, the movement causing her long, white blond curls to sway around her thin shoulders. "Santa wouldn't turn us in," she insisted. "Not before we have a chance to find our parents."

Pip groaned. "Kelsey, promise you won't tell him."

She heaved a long-suffering sigh. "Okay, I won't. But I *will* tell him we want to find our parents by Christmas!" she added with an uncharacteristic touch of defiance.

Pip nodded. "Okay, you can tell him that." It couldn't hurt, he decided.

It seemed to take hours before they finally reached the head of the line, though it couldn't have been more than thirty minutes. Pip shook his head at the elf-garbed woman who wanted to take their picture—only six dollars for a four-by-six instant snapshot in a commemorative folder, she told them brightly. He walked his sister to Santa's chair, then stood guard nearby as she climbed eagerly onto the man's velvet-covered knee.

Shrewd but kind green eyes studied Pip for a moment before turning to his giggling sister. "What's your name?" Santa asked her, his voice not booming and loud, as she'd expected, but warm and friendly.

"Kelsey Coleman," she replied, with just a hint of a reproving frown. "But I thought you'd know that already."

"Kelsey?" He seemed surprised as he peered at her through his tiny round glasses. "Goodness, how you've grown since last year! I hardly knew you."

Appeased, she giggled again. "I've grown about four inches," she informed him proudly. "And that's Pip," she added, waving a hand toward her brother. "He's grown feets and feets."

"Yes, he is much bigger than he was," Santa agreed, turning those intent eyes on Pip once again.

The boy shifted position, feeling a bit uncomfortable beneath the scrutiny. He was relieved when the white-bearded man turned his attention back to Kelsey.

"So, Kelsey," Santa said encouragingly, "what can I do for you this year?"

The little girl took a deep breath, clasped her tiny hands tightly in her lap and gazed up at him. "I only want our parents this year, Santa. I don't need any toys—well, not many, anyway," she amended carefully. "But mostly I just want our parents."

Santa blinked behind his lenses. "Your parents?"

She nodded fervently. "Not our *first* parents, of course. They're dead. But Pip says we can find new parents who will love us and take care of us and always let us be together. Aunt Opal and Aunt Essie don't really want us and they said they're going to split us up after Christmas, but me and Pip ain't going to let them. Pip says no one can split us up, especially after we find our new parents. Will you help us find them, Santa?"

Santa listened to every word of the child's artless rambling. Pip held his breath, regretting his sister's tendency to talk too much and hoping this Santa's helper wouldn't do or say the wrong thing. Kelsey was so easily crushed.

"You know, Kelsey," Santa said slowly, "I usually bring toys for Christmas, not parents."

She nodded, a bit disappointed with his answer.

He scratched his beard. "However…"

She brightened and looked up hopefully when he spoke again.

"I'll see what I can do," he said, gently squeezing her hands.

Pip thought his sister's smile was brighter than all the Christmas lights in the mall. "Thank you," she said, impulsively throwing her arms around the man's substantial waist. "Oh, thank you, Santa."

"Now, now, you must wait until afterward to thank me," he admonished. He reached into a nearby basket and plucked out two candy canes. "Here's a candy for you and one for your brother."

"Thank you," she said, hopping down from his lap. "When will we find our parents, Santa?"

"That remains to be seen. But in the meantime, have you seen the new doll shop upstairs on the third floor? I'm sure you'll enjoy it. It's one of my very favorites."

Kelsey's face lit up again. "A doll shop?"

Pip swallowed a groan, knowing where he'd have to take her next.

Santa patted the little girl's blond head, then looked at Pip. "You take very good care of your little sister, you hear?"

Pip nodded somberly. "I intend to, sir."

"Good. Oh, and you might want to look into the sporting-goods store across from the doll shop. There are some fascinating things to be found in sporting-goods stores these days."

Pip took Kelsey's hand. "Maybe I will."

He fancied that he could almost feel the warmth of the bearded man's smile as he and Kelsey walked away.

PIP NEARLY GAGGED when he saw the name of the doll shop. "Beautiful Babies?" he groaned. "Give me a break."

But Kelsey was still tugging at his hand. "I want to go in, Pip. Santa said it was his most-favorite store. Please? I just want to see it."

Pip couldn't hold out against her pleading eyes. He sighed manfully and allowed himself to be towed inside.

Kelsey was entranced from the moment she walked into the shop and saw the rows and rows of dolls. Baby dolls. Fashion dolls. Collector dolls. Handmade dolls. One-of-a-kind dolls. Pip could certainly understand why Kelsey liked the place; if he were a girl, he thought indulgently, he'd probably like it, too.

"Pip," Kelsey said in the high-pitched, breathless voice she reserved for very special excitement. *"Look."*

The doll was displayed at Kelsey's eye level. It had thick, curly dark hair, huge black eyes and a painted pink smile. It wore a pale blue dress with white lace, and tiny white shoes. Pip thought it was okay. Kelsey, apparently, thought it the most beautiful doll she'd ever seen.

"Oh," she whispered. "Can I pick it up, Pip? Please? I'll be very careful."

Pip checked the store. Other kids were holding dolls, admiring and cuddling them as their mothers watched or shopped. "Sure," he said. "You can hold her. But just for a minute."

Kelsey lifted the doll as though it were made of the most fragile glass rather than soft plastic. Such love shone from her eyes that Pip wondered if maybe he could buy her the doll for Christmas. He was already trying to decide how he could hide it from her when he saw the price tag dangling from one pink, plastic wrist.

He gulped. Even if he spent his whole life's savings of ten dollars and thirty-five cents, he couldn't come close to buying the doll for Kelsey.

"Uh, Kels? You'd better put it back," he urged. "You don't want to get it messed up or anything."

"I won't hurt her," Kelsey returned, cradling the doll against her little chest. "I just want to hold her for another minute."

A woman approached them from the back of the store. "You like that one?" she said encouragingly, her voice musical and friendly.

Pip expected Kelsey to answer. When she didn't, he looked around to see why. He found her staring open-mouthed at the woman, a look of shock on her baby face.

Frowning, he followed her gaze. He couldn't quite understand his sister's reaction. The woman was pretty— well, he supposed most people would call her beautiful. She had thick, wavy, shoulder-length dark hair that framed her face and moved when she did. Large, almost-black eyes surrounded by long, curling lashes. A little nose and a nice smile.

A pink smile, he realized. Just like the doll's.

He suddenly understood. The woman looked very much like the doll Kelsey had taken such a liking to. She was wearing a blue shirt with white lace at the collar, and a full blue skirt with lace pockets. She was even wearing white shoes—though hers were sneakers, not the shiny vinyl of the doll's shoes.

The woman was studying his sister with a curious smile. Probably wondering why Kelsey was looking at her as though she had two heads or something, Pip thought with a grimace.

He nudged his sister. "She thinks the doll's real pretty, ma'am," he said. "Put it back on the shelf, Kelsey."

Kelsey replaced the doll with visible reluctance, though she hardly took her eyes from the salesclerk.

Pip caught his sister's hand and tugged her toward another display. "Look over here," he said, hoping the woman would turn to another customer. "These dolls are dressed like fairy-tale characters. See, there's Cinderella and Snow White and—"

Kelsey suddenly regained her voice. "Pip!" she squeaked, clutching his arm. "That's her! That's my mom." She was still looking at the dark-haired woman, who'd turned to answer a question from a very pregnant customer.

Pip blinked. "Huh?"

"She's 'xactly what I wanted. She even looks like the doll."

"But, Kels—"

"It's her, Pip. Really. *That's* why Santa sent us to this shop. For her!"

"But—"

"Do you think we should tell her now? That we've picked her for our mom, I mean. Do you think she'll be excited? I am!"

That was obvious. Feeling as though the situation was rapidly getting out of hand, Pip tried to calm his sister, who was tugging eagerly at his hand again. "We can't just tell her that, Kels. We have to have a plan."

Since Kelsey had great respect for Pip's plans—after all, hadn't it been one of his plans that had brought them to this mall in search of parents?—she grew still and nodded gravely. "What plan?"

Darned if he knew. "Let's just watch her for a minute," he suggested in a conspiratorial murmur. "We want to be sure."

That seemed reasonable to Kelsey. They pretended great interest in the dolls while they crept closer to the sales desk, where the woman had gone to ring up a sale for the pregnant woman.

"Ryan, do we have any more of the red-and-green-plaid

wrapping paper?" a tall, red-haired woman behind the counter asked. "I can't find any."

The dark-haired saleslady turned to answer.

"Ryan," Kelsey whispered. "Her name is Ryan. Isn't that pretty?"

Pip had always considered that a boy's name himself, but he kept quiet, continuing to watch the woman who so fascinated his sister.

"It's been a madhouse today, hasn't it?" the redhead was asking, pretending to wipe her brow with one hand. "Why do I have the feeling we're going to be here very late tonight restocking and doing paperwork?"

"You don't have to stay very late," Ryan assured her. "I know Jack will be impatient for you to get home. I can handle most of it myself."

The redhead made a face. "You will not. I told you I'd help you get through the Christmas season and I will. Jack will understand. It's you I'm worried about. You're going to be so busy during the next month that you'll be lucky to have any social life at all."

Ryan shrugged. "What social life? It's not as if I'm dating anyone right now. Face it, Lynn, I'm a single in a doubles' season. I might as well be working instead of sitting at home watching old Christmas movies on cable."

Several customers approached the desk, their arms loaded with purchases. Both Ryan and the woman she'd called Lynn snapped to attention.

So she was a single lady. Could be a problem.

Pip took Kelsey's hand, figuring they'd lingered in the doll shop as long as they could without attracting undue attention. "C'mon," he murmured. "Let's go."

"But—"

"The plan," he reminded her when she hesitated. "We have to work out the plan."

She nodded and followed him out, with only one last, wistful look over her shoulder. Pip wasn't sure whether it was directed at the doll or the woman named Ryan. Maybe both.

Scratching his head, he looked around the crowded mall, as if in search of inspiration. He spotted the sporting-goods store across the way.

"There's the other shop Santa told us to visit," he exclaimed. "Maybe we'll get an idea while we're in there."

"Maybe that's where we'll find our dad," Kelsey agreed.

Pip wasn't so sure it would be that easy, but at least visiting the sporting-goods store would buy him some time to think.

During the past week, it had occurred to him that he and Kelsey could find the parents they'd been longing for at the mall—didn't the advertisements all say that you could find *anything* at the mall? Teeming with shoppers, the mall seemed a good place to look around, pick out some likely looking prospects.

He hadn't expected Kelsey to pick out a single lady. He'd sort of hoped for a set.

Kelsey was more interested in the store employees than in the merchandise so artfully displayed for Christmas browsers. She frowned.

"I don't think I like that one," she said, pointing to a scowling clerk behind the sales desk. The unpleasant-looking man was arguing with a customer about a return, and there was a vein throbbing in his skinny neck, as though he was really angry. "I don't want him for my dad," she stated flatly.

"Me, either," Pip agreed, eyeing the shopkeeper's soft-looking hands. Sissy hands. Probably never held a football in his life.

His attention was suddenly caught by someone who obviously knew exactly what to do with a football. He was standing ten feet from Pip and Kelsey, tossing a ball from one hand to another as though testing its feel.

He was a tall man who seemed to loom over the other

customers, at least from Pip's viewpoint. He had dark blond hair—rather like Pip's own—and eyes that might have been blue or gray. Pip couldn't tell which.

He had a dark tan—he was the outdoors type, apparently—and a strong chin. He was wearing a thick green sweater and very faded jeans, with what looked to Pip like real Western boots. His nose was just a little crooked, but Pip liked it.

As though sensing that someone was watching him, the man suddenly looked up. His gaze met Pip's. He smiled.

Kelsey's fingers tightened around Pip's hand. Pip squeezed absently, staring at the man's smile. Like his nose, it was a little crooked. But again Pip approved.

This, he thought, looked like a guy a kid wouldn't mind having for a dad.

The man tossed the ball into the air again, catching it neatly. "Looks like a good one, doesn't it?"

Pip nodded politely in response to the friendly question. "Yes, sir. That looks like a great ball."

"Glad to know you agree. I think I'll buy it."

Pip watched as the man made his way across the store to the unfriendly salesclerk.

"Well?" Kelsey whispered.

"Yeah," Pip murmured. "Maybe."

When the man left the sporting-goods store they were right on his heels, trying their best to blend into the shopping crowd so he wouldn't notice them. He went into a nearby ice-cream parlor, and Pip dug into his pocket for the ten-dollar bill.

"Want an ice-cream cone?" he asked Kelsey, who nodded eagerly.

A bubbly blond waitress and a more somber-looking older woman stood behind the counter. The man the children had been following headed straight for the blonde.

Pip placed his order with the other woman, watching the man out of the corner of his eye, trying to be as inconspicuous as possible.

The man was leaning on the counter, smiling that crooked smile at the blonde, who seemed to find it as appealing as Pip had.

"What can I do for you?" she asked, sounding to Pip a bit breathless.

"What do you recommend?" the man asked, leaning closer.

"How about a hot-fudge brownie supreme?" she suggested, batting her long eyelashes.

Pip thought she looked kind of goofy hanging all over the guy like that. Personally, he preferred the dark-haired woman in the doll shop to this one. He didn't think he'd care for a mom who giggled and twirled her hair.

The man flirted with the waitress a few more minutes before making his selection. Pip and Kelsey already had their ice-cream cones and were sitting at a tiny round table, eating and watching.

"Here you go," the waitress said, sliding a towering concoction of fudge, ice cream and whipping cream across the counter to the man. "What's your name, anyway?" she asked a bit too casually.

"Max. What's yours?"

"Brittany. Do you play football?" she asked, nodding toward the ball he held under one arm.

"Some of my buddies get together and play most Sunday afternoons at City Park. Come by some time," he said. "We can always use another player."

Brittany giggled. "I don't much like to play, but maybe I'll be a cheerleader."

Pip groaned.

Max only nodded. "See you around, Brittany."

He carried his ice cream to a small table not far from the one Pip and Kelsey had chosen. He caught Pip's eyes, paused a moment as though in surprised recognition, then smiled and turned his attention to his ice cream.

Max, Pip thought reflectively. *Nice name.*

He wondered how Max felt about video games and Batman.

Pip and Kelsey finished their cones before Max had half finished his own treat. Still trying to be inconspicuous, they went out into the mall and pretended to look into shop windows until he finally emerged.

They watched as he roamed aimlessly around the mall, tossing the football from hand to hand and stopping occasionally to peer into a window. Both Pip and Kelsey were excited when Max walked past the doll shop, stopped, looked back over his shoulder and then went inside.

"He's in there with *her!*" Kelsey squealed. "Come on, Pip, let's go watch."

Pip bit his lower lip, torn between caution and curiosity. Curiosity won out.

"Okay," he said. "But stay quiet and don't call attention to us, you hear?"

"Okay, Pip," Kelsey said absently, her little sneakers already moving toward Beautiful Babies.

2

MAX MONROE FELT more than a bit out of place in the doll shop. He tucked the new football more snugly beneath his arm and wandered through the crowded aisles, eyeing the rows of smiling plastic faces and wondering how a person went about selecting one. Should he just grab the first doll that caught his eye? Were certain dolls more appropriate than others for a girl of a certain age? How was a guy supposed to know these things?

He looked around for help.

A dark-haired, dark-eyed woman was already headed his way, wearing a plastic name tag with a doll's face painted on it identifying her as a store employee. She smiled, and Max promptly forgot why he'd come in.

Nice smile, he thought. *Nice face. Great body. A particularly nice left hand. No rings.*

"May I help you find something?" she asked, and her voice was more musical than the Christmas carols that filled the air.

He gave her his best helpless-male smile. "I could certainly use some assistance," he assured her. *Especially from you,* he added silently.

"Are you looking for a gift?"

"A Christmas present for my niece." He checked the woman's name tag as he spoke. Ryan Clark. The word *owner* was printed in small letters beneath her name.

"How old is your niece?" Ryan Clark asked him.

Max had to think a minute. "Five? Six, maybe."

"You aren't sure?"

With a rueful shrug, he shook his head. "My sister and her family live in Hawaii. I don't get to see them often, I'm afraid. But I'm pretty sure Jenny is five."

"I see. Well, maybe a baby doll would be most appropriate. Little girls of all ages love something they can cuddle."

Max liked the sound of that. He took a step closer. "Yeah. Something to cuddle sounds good to me."

Ryan Clark shot him a suspicious look and took a step backward.

"For my niece, of course," he added hastily.

Oops. Wrong approach with this one. The blonde at the ice-cream parlor would have responded with a blush and a giggle. Max actually preferred the stern reproval in Ryan Clark's dark eyes. He always enjoyed a challenge.

"Of course," she said, her voice now a bit chilly.

"Ryan, could you give me a hand here for a minute?" a harried-looking redhead called out from the sales counter, which was surrounded by impatient shoppers.

Ryan waved an acknowledgment. "Perhaps you'd like to look around a bit," she suggested to Max. "The baby dolls are in that section. I'll check back with you in a few minutes."

"Sure, take your time," he said magnanimously. "I'm in no hurry."

He watched her full skirt sway around her very nice legs as she walked away. "No hurry at all," he murmured.

Without much interest, he roamed the shop, stopping occasionally to study one doll or another. Frankly, they all looked pretty much alike to him.

He glanced at a few price tags and grew even more puzzled. Why were some of them ten bucks and others several hundred dollars? Who the hell could tell the difference?

A dark-haired doll in a blue-and-white dress caught his eye, and he chuckled. Funny. The doll reminded him a bit of Ryan Clark.

He bent to pick the doll up and found himself face-to-face with a little girl with white blond curls and enormous blue eyes. She was studying him so intently that he felt compelled to say something.

"I'm buying a gift for my niece," he said. "She's about your age. Do you think she would like this doll?"

"No," the child answered positively, shaking her head. She pointed toward a round-faced baby doll dressed in frothy lace. "That one's much better," she said earnestly. "You should buy that one."

Amused, Max replaced the dark-haired doll and picked up the other one. "This one, huh?" he asked, noting that the prices were comparable.

The tot nodded. "That's a much better one for your niece."

"Then I'd better buy it, hadn't I?"

He grinned at the look of relief that crossed the child's face when she glanced at the dark-haired doll. The little girl returned his smile with a particularly sweet one of her own and then disappeared into the crowds around her. Max assumed she'd returned to her mother's side. He'd bet the kid would be urging her mom to hurry and buy the dark-haired doll for her before some other inconsiderate shopper snapped it up.

Kids, Max thought with an indulgent shake of his head. They were cute, but weird. He would never figure them out.

All in all, it was a good thing he'd long since decided he would never have any of his own.

"HE'S GORGEOUS," Lynn Patterson whispered as she and Ryan both finished ringing up their sales. "What does he want?"

Ryan followed her assistant's gaze to the tall, blond man in the green sweater, who was studying a display of clown dolls. "He said he wants a gift for his niece."

"Niece? Not daughter?"

"Something tells me this guy doesn't have any kids,"

Ryan said wryly, remembering how blank he'd been when she'd asked his niece's age.

"Then he's probably single. What are you waiting for, Ryan? Get over there and offer assistance to the man. *Personal* assistance."

"Lynn," Ryan groaned.

"C'mon, look at him. He's amazing. That hair. Those eyes. Those shoulders. He looks like…like—"

"Like a heartbreaker," Ryan said flatly.

"Well, yeah," Lynn admitted. "But what a way to go."

Ryan's attention had already wandered. "Lynn, do you see those two kids over there? The boy and girl?"

"Hmm. Cute, aren't they?"

"They've been hanging around in here for quite a while. I don't think they're with anyone. Help me keep an eye on them, okay?"

Lynn frowned. "You think they'd try to steal something? At their age?"

Ryan sighed. "Unfortunately, it's a possibility. They're starting younger these days."

Her gaze wandered back to the children. They really were cute kids. The boy hovered protectively over his little sister, watching her so carefully. And the girl was an adorable moppet, curly haired, big eyed, pink cheeked. Their clothes were faded and worn, and there was something about them that made Ryan feel a bit sad.

She couldn't define it. But there was something…

"I've decided to get this one."

The blond heartbreaker leaned against the counter, a lace-clad baby doll clutched in one hand and the football she'd noticed earlier in the other. He was giving her that sexy, crooked smile again—the one that made her insides quiver even though she told herself it was ridiculous to react that way.

Lynn, she noted wryly, had suddenly—and deliberately, Ryan was sure—disappeared.

Keeping her expression as polite as possible, she reached for the doll in the man's hand. "This is a nice selection. I'm sure your niece will love it."

"I hope so. I had some assistance from an expert," he said with a grin, nodding over his shoulder.

Following his gesture, she saw the little blond girl and her brother. Ryan smiled, then turned to the cash register. "Will this be all?"

"For now," he murmured, making the words sound as though they had another meaning.

She didn't even blink; she simply rang up the purchase and gave him the total. He handed her a gold credit card.

"My name's Max Monroe," he said unnecessarily. "I have some more shopping to do and then I thought I'd grab an early dinner in the Mexican restaurant downstairs. Will you join me?"

"Thank you, but no. I have to work," she explained. She wasn't exactly surprised by the invitation, but she still felt a bit flustered by it.

He lifted an eyebrow. "You'll have time to eat, won't you?"

She shook her head. "It's one of the busiest shopping days of the season. I won't be able to take off any time this evening."

"Then how about a late dinner? After your shop closes, I mean."

"Thank you again, but no."

"Some other time, maybe?"

She gave him a vague smile. "If you'll excuse me," she murmured, nodding to the two women who'd just come up behind him, their arms loaded with dolls and accessories. "I have to tend to my other customers now."

Max didn't look particularly disappointed—not that she'd expected him to. She was sure he could find any number of women in the mall who'd dearly love to "grab an early dinner" with him. She just didn't happen to be one of them.

He gave her a jaunty salute, tucked the bag holding the

doll under his arm with the football and sauntered out of the shop.

Ryan was aware of several long, appreciative sighs from customers in her shop who'd watched him leave. She was also well aware of the frown of disapproval she was getting from her assistant. She suspected that Lynn had overheard the invitation, and Ryan's refusal. She knew she'd be hearing about it later.

But for now, she had a shop to run.

"OH, MAN," Pip groaned outside the doll shop. "He crashed and burned."

"What does that mean?" Kelsey asked innocently.

"Never mind." He sighed. Things had looked so promising for a minute there.

"There he goes," Kelsey whispered, pointing toward the glass elevator in the center of the mall. "Our dad's getting away."

Pip looked at his Batman digital watch and frowned. "We have to be going, too."

"But, Pip—"

"It's getting late, Kels. You don't want to get caught, do you?"

She shook her head.

"Okay, let's go then. We'll come back tomorrow."

That cheered her some. "Can we see our mom again tomorrow? And my doll?"

"Sure."

"And Santa?"

"Again?"

"Yes. There's something else I want to tell him."

Pip sighed heavily. Caring for a little girl was such a responsibility, he thought somberly. "We'll see. Okay?"

"Okay, Pip." She slipped her hand into his.

Together they headed for the same elevator the man named Max had used only minutes before.

ON SATURDAY the mall was as crowded as it had been the previous day. It took Max nearly twenty minutes to find a parking space when he arrived early that afternoon. Not that he particularly minded cruising the parking lot watching the shoppers; it wasn't as if he had anything better to do.

He should probably be working, but he wasn't in the mood today. To the dismay of his agent and editors, who considered him the worst case of wasted potential they'd ever known, he was all too rarely in the mood to work.

Max was bored—certainly not an unfamiliar condition for him. Problem was, there'd been few challenges lately in his self-indulgent, hedonistic, freedom-above-all-else life-style. And he thrived on challenges. Which was the reason he'd headed back to the mall today.

A brisk wind was blowing, reminding him that winter was definitely at hand. He tucked his leather driving gloves into a pocket of his bomber jacket and pulled the collar higher around his neck. His thick, dark gold hair blew slightly in the wind. He stepped beneath the mall awning and ran a hand through the heavy strands, letting them fall haphazardly into place.

A heavyset woman with a bad complexion and a sweet smile stood beside a collection box patiently ringing a handbell, her nose red from the wind. Her chubby hands were pink with cold and callused from years of abuse. Max dug in his jeans pocket, pulled out a ten-dollar bill and slipped it into the collection box.

"Bless you, sir. And Merry Christmas to ya," the woman said brightly.

"Cool day, isn't it?" he asked her.

Still smiling, she nodded. "It certainly is. Your donation will help buy blankets and warm food for those that don't have 'em."

On impulse, Max pulled out his leather gloves and pressed them into the woman's free hand. "Wear these," he urged. "You don't want your hand to freeze to that bell handle," he added lightly.

She blinked in surprise. "But—"

"Merry Christmas," he said as he walked away, feeling uncomfortable with his gesture.

"Thank you, sir. God bless you," she called after him, already tugging the soft gloves over her rough hands.

Max blended into the crowd of people pushing their way through the mall entrance. He'd have to pick up a new pair of gloves, he thought. He hadn't really liked the way the others fit, anyway.

The same Christmas carols he'd heard yesterday poured from overhead speakers, blending with the jabber of constantly moving shoppers. The enticing aroma of fresh-baked chocolate-chip cookies drifted from a Mrs. Field's shop, blending with the scents of cinnamon and evergreen and peppermint from Christmas displays.

A frowning, forty-something woman bumped Max's arm and dropped her packages. He helped her retrieve them, flirted with her for a moment, then moved away, leaving her smiling.

"Hey, Max. How's it goin'?"

The call made Max look around. He nodded when he spotted an acquaintance walking his way. "Hi, Stan. Doing some shopping?"

A stocky African-American of about Max's age, Stan carried a chubby baby in a backpack and held the hand of a little boy who might have been three or four.

"The wife dragged me down here," Stan admitted with a grimace. "She's in J.C. Penney's now. I told her I'd take the kids to ride the Christmas train while she shopped. Standing in a line full of whining kids beats the hell out of watching her choose a flannel nightgown for her sister."

Max laughed. "I feel for you, pal."

"You don't know what you're missing staying single, buddy."

"Whatever it is, I'm getting along just fine without it," Max quipped.

"You just wait. Someday I'm going to find *you* in the mall with a wife and a half-dozen kids, and then I'm going to be the one laughing my butt off."

"No way, Stan. Trust me."

"Mmm." Stan grinned, apparently unconvinced. "You playing tomorrow?" he asked as his son tugged impatiently at his hand.

"Yeah, probably. You?"

"I'll be there."

"Daddy. Train," the little boy insisted.

Stan sighed. "Gotta go. See you tomorrow."

"Yeah. See ya', Stan." Max watched the trio move away, then shook his head sympathetically. Poor guy.

He headed again for the escalators. His winding path took him past the gingerbread house in the center of the mall, where a long line of ankle-biters waited to sit on Santa's plump lap. Now *there* was a nightmare of a temporary job, Max thought with a shudder. He wondered how many times a day Santa's lap got soaked by leaky toddlers.

As if he'd heard Max's thoughts, the white-bearded, red-suited man glanced his way. Their gazes held for a moment. The older man smiled and nodded, almost as if they'd met before.

Max returned the nod and told himself the guy was just doing his job, spreading Christmas cheer among the shoppers to make them more inclined to spend their money. He moved on, though he had the odd sensation that he was being watched as he shuffled onto the escalator between an elderly woman and three giggling teenage girls.

RYAN WAS TAKING a lunch break in the mall food court on the ground floor. She sat alone at one end of a long table, a fast-food salad in front of her.

She would have worked straight through the day, but

business had slowed a bit during the past hour and Lynn had insisted she take a break. Lynn was sometimes fussier than an old mother hen, but now that Ryan was sitting down, she was glad she'd let her assistant talk her into the respite.

She took a long, appreciative sip of her iced tea, then opened a packet of low-fat ranch dressing and squeezed some onto her salad. She had just stabbed her plastic fork into a crisp chunk of lettuce when someone slid into the seat directly across the table from her.

She glanced up and was glad she hadn't yet started to eat. She was quite sure she would have choked.

"Mind if I join you?" Max Monroe asked, smiling across the table at her as he unwrapped a bacon double cheeseburger.

It annoyed her that she remembered his name. It irritated her that he had found her now, when there was little she could do to avoid him. And most of all, it made her absolutely furious that the sight of his unruly, gold-streaked hair and ridiculously crooked grin made her go all breathless and quivery like some awestruck adolescent.

She took a deep breath, had a stern mental talk with her hormones and gave him a cool shrug. "It's an open food court," she said. "You can sit wherever you like."

Unfazed by her less-than-gracious reply, Max arranged his meal in front of him—the burger, a large order of fries, a jug-size soft drink and a deep-fried apple pie. Glancing from the high-calorie, high-everything-else food to his slim, firm waist, Ryan wondered jealously if he routinely ate that way, and if so, where did it all go.

She took another bite of her low-calorie, low-fat, low-taste salad, finding less pleasure in it than she would have a few minutes earlier.

"Didn't we meet yesterday in the doll shop upstairs?" he asked, though she suspected he remembered their meeting as well as she did.

She gave him a polite, deliberately distant smile. "Yes, I believe we did."

"In case you've forgotten, I'm Max Monroe. And you're Ryan, right?"

"Ryan Clark." She made no pretense at being flattered that he'd remembered.

"How's business today?" he asked, after swallowing a hefty bite of his sandwich.

She concentrated on her salad—or pretended to. "Busy."

"That's good, isn't it?"

"Yes, of course." She wondered why he was wasting time talking to her when she was making it obvious that she wasn't interested.

At least, she was trying not to be interested.

Okay, the guy was gorgeous. His knock-your-socks-off smile made her toes curl.

If she'd run into him even a year earlier, she'd probably have bantered right back at him, maybe thrown a few passes of her own. She'd have been open to the possibility of a frivolous flirtation, maybe a light-hearted, unquestionably temporary affair—though such encounters had been extremely rare for her. A year ago, she'd been busy preparing to open her business. She hadn't been ready for a serious relationship, though she might have made time for a bit of fun with a man like Max, had one come along.

But that had been then, and things had changed. Her life was moving along exactly the way she'd planned, and a brief fling didn't fit in with her new goals. Now it was time to get serious about looking for Mr. Right.

She would almost have bet her precious shop that it would be a complete waste of energy to expect anything permanent with a man like Max Monroe. If she was going to start a family before she reached thirty, there wasn't time to get distracted by a charming heartbreaker.

She looked up and her gaze met Max's. His smile crinkled the corners of his blue-gray eyes with tiny lines that hinted at hours spent in the sun. It made her want to smile back at him. It also made her think of fun and laughter and lighthearted conversation and teeth-rattling lovemaking.

If only she'd met him a year or so ago, she thought wistfully. Back when she'd still had time to have her teeth rattled a bit.

Her iced tea splashed precariously against the sides of the paper cup when the table was suddenly jarred from close by. Both Ryan and Max grabbed their drinks to prevent them from spilling. Ryan looked down, not quite sure if she was relieved or disappointed that the spell that had fallen when her eyes locked with Max's had been abruptly broken.

Two children, a boy and a smaller girl, were just sliding into seats close to Ryan and Max. The boy flushed and looked sheepish when he saw that Ryan was looking at him. "Sorry," he said. "I stumbled against the table."

"That's okay," she assured him. "No harm done."

She started to turn away, then hesitated when she noticed the little girl across the table from the boy. Big blue eyes. A mop of white blond curls. A Cupid's bow of a mouth. And the boy—sandy haired, with blue eyes that looked surprisingly shrewd for his age and a no-nonsense little chin that would one day be formidable.

She'd seen them before, she realized. Yesterday, in her shop.

The little girl was smiling at her. Ryan instinctively returned the smile, which made the child giggle.

"Kelsey," the boy murmured, handing his little sister a decorated box that held a McDonald's Happy Meal. "Settle down and eat your lunch."

Ryan glanced at Max, who was watching her with a grin. She knew he was as amused—and bemused—as she by the boy's overly mature manner. She smiled wryly back at him.

"Look at what I got in my Happy Meal, Pip," the child

he'd called Kelsey said, holding up a molded-plastic figure. "Minnie Mouse!"

"Yeah, that's cool," her brother said, taking a bite of his own small cheeseburger. "Hang on to it or you'll lose it."

Kelsey clutched the toy more firmly in her chubby hand. "I won't lose it."

"Eat your lunch, now."

"Okay, Pip." The little girl obediently took an enormous mouthful of her own burger.

Biting the inside of her lip to avoid laughing, Ryan wondered if the children were eating alone while their mother shopped. They seemed awfully young to be wandering through a crowded mall on their own.

She remembered that they had seemed unaccompanied the day before, in her shop, and she shook her head slightly in disapproval of their parents' negligence. She would have liked to chat with the children, but didn't want to encourage them to talk to strangers.

Max apparently didn't consider that precaution. "You guys doing some Christmas shopping?" he asked encouragingly.

"You might say that," the boy answered after a momentary consideration.

His sister giggled at a private joke.

"Been to see Santa yet?"

Kelsey nodded avidly. "Twice. I forgot to tell him something the first time, so I went back. He remembered me. He said he would—"

"Kelsey!" Pip said patiently. "It was a yes-or-no question."

"Oh. Then, yes. We seen him."

"Saw him," Pip murmured.

Kelsey gave a deep sigh. "Saw him," she repeated.

"Didn't I see you in my shop yesterday?" Ryan asked, forgetting her own mental warnings about talking to the kids.

"The doll shop," Kelsey said, nodding again. "I like your store very much."

"It's a cool shop," her brother agreed politely. "If you like dolls, I guess," he couldn't resist adding.

Ryan laughed. "I happen to like dolls."

"Me, too," Kelsey seconded fervently.

"Feel free to come back in and look around whenever you like," Ryan said, touched by the child's obvious delight in the shop. She had never gotten over her own childhood fascination with dolls of any shape and size, so she could easily identify with her.

Kelsey looked pleased by the invitation. "Thank you. Maybe Pip will let me come look again after lunch."

The boy nodded, still concentrating on his hamburger.

"I remember you," Max said suddenly, looking at the girl. "You helped me pick out a doll for my niece yesterday."

The child smiled shyly. "My name's Kelsey," she volunteered. "That's my brother. His name is Peter, but I call him Pip, 'cause I like Pip better."

"Hello, Kelsey. Hi, Pip. I'm Max."

The children acknowledged his greeting, then turned expectantly to Ryan.

"I'm Ryan," she said obligingly.

"I'm six years old." Kelsey made the announcement with pride. "Pip's nine."

"I'm thirty-four," Max said gravely. "How old are *you*, Ryan?"

She gave him a pointed look. "I'm twenty-eight."

"Are you married, Ryan?" Kelsey asked innocently.

"No," she said, forcing a smile. "I'm not married."

"Are *you* married, Max?" Pip asked casually.

"No," Max answered, still looking amused. "How about you, Pip? Tied the knot yet?"

Kelsey dissolved into giggles. "He's not married, silly," she said reprovingly. "He's only a kid—even if he is a lot older than me."

"Oh, that's right. I guess I forgot for a minute," Max said, winking at Ryan.

She reached desperately for her iced tea, wondering in exasperation how a crooked grin and a quick wink could raise her body temperature by about fifty degrees.

"We saw you in the sporting-goods store, too," Pip told Max. "You bought a football. Have you played with it yet?"

Max chuckled. "Not yet. I'll probably try it out on Sunday. Some of my friends and I get together on Sunday afternoons to play touch football in City Park."

"City Park's not far from where we live," Kelsey commented. "Me and Pip go there sometimes and play on the swings. I like to swing."

A mall employee in a bright red-and-green uniform approached the table with a colorful bouquet of helium-filled balloons bobbing behind her.

"Hi," she said, her ponytail bouncing perkily. She looked at Ryan. "Would your kids like a balloon? They're free."

"Oh, uh…" Flustered, Ryan looked at the children.

"I'd like one, thank you," Kelsey said, pointing to a red balloon. "May I have that one?"

"Sure." The young woman plucked the red balloon from the batch and pressed the string into Kelsey's hand. "Don't let go now or it'll fly away. Maybe your dad'll tie it to your wrist."

Before anyone could answer, she turned to Pip. "How about you? Want a balloon?"

Pip shook his head. "No, thank you."

"Okay. See ya, then. Have a nice day."

The young woman had already spotted another family group. As she moved toward them, she looked over her shoulder at Ryan. "Nice kids," she said.

Fortunately, Ryan was spared having to answer.

Kelsey was grinning at Max. "She thought you were my daddy."

"Yeah. I guess she did." Max looked almost as disconcerted as Ryan had felt when the woman had mistaken her for the children's mother.

"You don't have any children, do you, Max?"

"No, Kelsey. I don't have any children."

The child gave him a melting smile. "Would you *like* some?"

She jerked suddenly, as though she'd been kicked beneath the table. "Ouch, Pip! That—"

"Finish your french fries," her brother said quickly. "You don't want them to get cold."

Kelsey sighed and turned back to her meal. "How can I eat and hold my balloon at the same time?"

"Here," Max said. "I'll tie it to your wrist for you."

Kelsey obligingly held out her hand. "Thank you, Max," she said with a coquettish bat of her eyes.

To Ryan's amusement, Max's cheeks darkened. "Yeah. Sure," he said, hastily tying the string into a loose slipknot.

Ryan gathered her empty plastic salad bowl and other trash, then pushed her chair away from the table. "I have to get back to work. It's been nice chatting with you, Kelsey and Pip."

"And Max," Kelsey reminded her.

"Yes, of course. And Max, too."

Max looked as though he wanted to say something else. Ryan hurried away before he had the chance.

Though she couldn't have explained her overreaction, she was still a bit shaken at being taken for a family with Max and the children. The experience had left an oddly hollow feeling deep inside her.

Must have been the salad, she decided. One could never trust fast-food places to have really fresh vegetables.

3

THE ESCALATORS WERE mobbed, and the glass elevators in the center of the mall were packed like sardine cans, with more shoppers waiting to get on. Ryan ducked into one of the discreetly located service elevators tucked into an out-of-the-way nook. She noticed as the doors closed silently behind her that she wasn't the only occupant.

Santa Claus was also on board.

"Taking a break?" she asked, pushing the button for the third floor.

"A brief one," Santa replied, his voice deep and pleasant, just the way Ryan thought it should be. "Did you have a nice lunch?"

Ryan wondered if he'd noticed her downstairs or was simply making a guess. "Yes, thank you. It's crazy this week, isn't it? I've noticed you've had some incredibly long lines of children waiting to see you."

"I don't mind. I love children."

"So do I," Ryan answered, unable to keep a touch of wistfulness out of her voice.

The elevator jerked oddly. Ryan steadied herself against the shiny metal wall. "What was that?"

"I'm not sure…."

The elevator stopped. Unfortunately, they had already passed the second floor and had not yet reached the third.

"Oh, no," Ryan groaned, pushing the third-floor button. Nothing happened. The car remained solidly wedged between floors.

On one of her most hectic business days, she was stuck in a service elevator. With Santa Claus. She groaned again.

"Now what do we do?" she asked aloud, as much to herself as to her companion.

"Push the red alarm button," the bearded man suggested kindly. "That will alert someone that there's a problem."

Ryan obliged, though she couldn't imagine anyone actually hearing the muted buzz over the frenzied commotion of the mall. They could be trapped in here for hours. She pulled at the high neckline of her Christmas-motif sweater, wondering if the elevator contained enough air.

"You don't suffer from claustrophobia, I hope," Santa said, watching her closely.

She managed a weak smile and shook her head. "I never have before."

"That's good. I'm afraid I have little experience dealing with hysteria."

Ryan lifted her chin. "I never," she said precisely, "get hysterical."

His smile was almost hidden by his lush, white, amazingly realistic-looking beard. "What a relief."

Ryan mechanically pushed the alarm button again. "I don't suppose you have Rudolph trained to rescue you in cases like this," she said inanely, trying to distract herself from noticing how small the car actually was, or how the walls seemed to be inching a bit closer to her.

"I'm afraid not. But I'm sure maintenance workers are already on the way. In the meantime, why don't we introduce ourselves? I'm Santa Claus."

Ryan laughed wryly. "Yes, I know. And I'm Ryan Clark."

"You work in the lovely doll shop on the third floor."

"I own it," she acknowledged. "You've been in?"

"Oh, I know all the best toy stores. Yours is delightful. I've recommended it to several shoppers."

"Why, thank you."

"You're welcome. And now, since we seem to have a few spare moments on our hands, why don't you tell Santa what *you* would like for Christmas?"

Her smile deepened. His calm, cheerful attitude relaxed her, making her realize there wasn't any real reason for panic.

"I want to have a successful, profitable season for my shop," she replied in answer to his frivolous question.

He frowned and shook his head, the fluffy white ball at the tip of his red cap bouncing with the movement. "I wasn't talking about business," he answered, reproving her gently. "I was asking about your true heart's desire. That's what the Christmas season is all about, after all."

"My heart's desire?" Ryan repeated, taken aback by his quaint phrasing. "I, er—"

"Surely there's something you want very badly. A cruise, perhaps? A trip to Europe?"

"I've seen Europe. I lived there for a year."

"Ah. So, what *would* you like?"

Ryan shrugged. She could hardly tell him that she had everything she wanted—with one quite notable exception.

She told herself that it was only the season making her so painfully aware of her single state. So many of her friends were looking for the perfect gift for their mate, making holiday plans for their children, anticipating the Christmas-morning rituals. Ryan was just feeling a bit left out, that was all.

Not something she could admit to a shopping-mall Santa Claus. No one, except maybe Lynn, knew how badly Ryan longed to find the right mate and start a family.

She wanted love. And commitment. A lifetime pledge. Babies. Deep, soul-warming contentment.

For some reason she thought of Max Monroe, with his take-me-if-you-dare smile and don't-expect-too-much-from-me eyes. For a man like Max, *marriage* was a four-letter word—like *jail*. Or *hell*.

Santa was watching her with an enigmatic smile. "Love

isn't such a difficult thing to ask for, Ryan," he said, making her stare at him in surprise. "It's taking a risk on it that's hard for most people," he added gently. "All you have to do is open yourself up to possibilities and be ready to act when the opportunity presents itself."

"I'll—" she swallowed "—I'll keep that in mind."

She wondered if he was putting her on, or if he'd been spending too much time in his Santa suit. Maybe his hat was too tight. Or maybe he'd watched *Miracle on 34th Street* a few too many times.

The older man chuckled. "What a cynic you are," he chided, but his tone was good-natured. She assumed he was responding to her expression, since she was reasonably confident that even the "real" Santa's talents didn't extend to mind reading.

Her companion reached into a deep pocket of his red velvet jacket and pulled out a peppermint cane. He extended it to her with an old-fashioned flourish. "For you," he said.

She took the candy with a weak smile. "Thank you."

"You're welcome."

The elevator suddenly hummed, jerked again and then started upward.

Ryan smiled in relief. "We're moving!"

The car stopped on the third floor. The doors slid silently, efficiently open. Ryan stepped out and drew a deep breath of fresh mall air.

She turned to look questioningly at Santa, who hadn't moved. "Aren't you getting out?"

He smiled. "No. There are children waiting for me downstairs. Have a nice day, Miss Clark. And don't forget about those possibilities."

The elevator closed before she could answer.

Ryan stared in bemusement at the metal doors, the candy cane gripped in one hand. And then she shook her head. "Weird," she murmured, turning away.

She put the incident out of her mind as she hurried back to her shop. She had many hours of hard work ahead of her. No more time to waste on silly fantasies.

PIP AND KELSEY CAME IN to visit the doll shop after their lunch, as Ryan had invited them to do. From behind the counter, Ryan smiled a greeting, though she was busy with a customer and didn't have time to chat. She noticed that Kelsey stopped in front of the dark-haired doll at the front of the shop, the one that had so fascinated the little girl the day before.

The children didn't stay long. By the time Ryan had a break and could have spoken to them, they were gone.

She busied herself behind the counter, picking up a jumble of shopping bags she'd dropped during a busy time earlier.

Her assistant suddenly tugged on her shoulder, urging her to stand upright. "He's back," Lynn said in an urgent whisper. "And oh, Lordy, he's even more gorgeous today than he was yesterday."

Following Lynn's excited gaze, Ryan swallowed hard when she saw that Max Monroe had just ambled through the open door. She moistened her lips and then frowned at her grinning assistant. "Would you stop it? How would Jack feel about you ogling the customers, hmm?"

Lynn giggled. "He'd approve if he knew I was only doing it for your benefit."

"Yeah, right."

Max didn't pause, but continued to the counter, where Lynn and Ryan waited on customers. "Hi again," he said.

"Looking for a present for another niece, Mr. Monroe?" Ryan asked as Lynn moved discreetly away.

"No."

Glancing around to make sure no one was listening, he leaned a bit closer to her. "Actually, I'm here to ask you for a date. Maybe we could see a movie or something?"

"Max—"

He touched her hand as it lay on the counter between them, giving her a look that made her voice fade. "I don't mean to annoy you with my persistence, but I thought I'd try this one more time. I like the way you smile, Ryan Clark. I'd like to get to know you. I guess that sounds like a line to you—"

"Yes," she admitted a bit shakily. "It does."

"Sorry. But it's true. Will you go out with me?"

"I—it's such a busy time for me," she said, wondering why she couldn't just tell him no.

For some reason, she kept hearing the voice of the mall Santa Claus. "All you have to do is open yourself up to possibilities and be ready to act when the opportunity presents itself," he'd said.

Maybe she'd leapt to conclusions about Max Monroe. Maybe she'd written him off as a "possibility" without giving him a fair chance. Maybe he wasn't really a heart-breaker, after all.

And maybe pigs would fly, she thought, eyeing the devil-ish twinkle in his blue-gray eyes.

"Just a movie," he said again, his fingers tightening on hers. "There's a nine-twenty feature in the theater down-stairs. I can meet you here at nine when you close your shop and we can see the film without even leaving the mall, if that makes you more comfortable. C'mon, Ryan. It'll be fun."

She felt something give inside her. "All right," she heard herself saying cautiously. "I guess it would be fun to see a movie. I haven't had a night off in a while."

His smile was blinding. "Great. Afterward, maybe we could have a cappuccino or something?"

"Let's just wait and see about afterward, okay?"

He nodded, accepting her equivocation without protest. "Then I'll meet you at nine?"

"Fine," she said, hoping she wasn't making a big mistake. But how bad could it be? If he'd been trying to put her at ease by choosing a safe, very public setting for their first date, he'd succeeded.

She suspected that he was entirely too good at this sort of thing. She'd have to be on her guard against him. But, still, she found herself looking forward to the evening.

It really *had* been too long since she'd had a night out, she reminded herself. That was all there was to it.

Max didn't linger, but left the shop looking quite satisfied with himself.

A plump matron with improbably red hair set a Barbie doll and several accessories on the counter in front of Ryan. "If a man like that had flirted with me that way while I was young and single, I know what I would have done," she murmured to her shopping companion with a wistful sigh, making no effort to keep Ryan from overhearing. "I'd have latched on to him before he'd known what had him."

Ryan flushed, busying herself immediately with ringing up the woman's purchases.

"Not many like him come along," the woman's friend agreed heartily. "Did you see that smile? If I were ten years younger, I'd chase him down right now."

The red-haired shopper snorted. "Fifteen years, maybe," she muttered.

Business quickly became brisk again, to Ryan's relief. She didn't want time to dwell on the evening ahead.

SHE THOUGHT OF little Kelsey at a quarter to nine that evening. Ryan was straightening the shelves, returning merchandise to its proper position, setting out a few new items in inviting poses, preparing for the next day's business, when she spotted the dark-haired doll. Smiling, she picked it up and fluffed its full blue skirt.

It was a pretty little thing, a numbered, limited edition from one of Ryan's favorite sources. It was the only one like it she had received, and she had actually expected it to sell before this.

She wished Kelsey's mother would come into the shop so Ryan could mention to her how much the little girl seemed to want the doll. Maybe Kelsey had already told her.

And then Ryan remembered the children's shabby clothing. She frowned. It was entirely possible their mother couldn't afford the doll.

Ryan set it back in its place, telling herself that if Kelsey's mother did come in, she would give her a very good deal. In this case, for Kelsey's sake, she was willing to forgo her profit.

There was something about that child that had gotten to Ryan. Pip, too.

When she looked up, she saw that Max had arrived for their impromptu date, and everything else left her mind.

IT WAS SOMETIME DURING the latter half of the movie that Ryan realized she'd been right to be suspicious of Max's seemingly innocuous manner in asking her out.

Oh, he'd started out casually enough. Escorted her into the theater as easily as if they'd known each other for years. Bought soft drinks and a huge tub of popcorn for them to share. Chatted about trivialities during the few minutes they waited before the feature started. Laughed along with her at the antics of the mixed-up couple falling in love on the screen.

He'd waited until she was relaxed and at ease with him before making his move—which he did with a subtlety and skill that would have made the teenage boys surrounding them green with envy. Ryan couldn't even have said when he scooted closer to her in his seat or when his arm slipped behind her.

At first she thought it coincidence that his hand brushed hers so often as she reached for popcorn. A very pleasant coincidence. And then she noticed how long his fingers lingered, making her all too vividly aware of the feel of him.

His thigh pressed lightly against hers, and she felt his warmth through the thin layers of clothing that separated them. His strength. Their shoulders touched; she felt him breathing. She could see his shadowed profile from the corner of her eye. His lashes were long, his chin firm, his mouth luscious.

Gorgeous. And dangerous.

The beautiful couple on screen eased into a slow, heated embrace. The background music was deep, stirring, swelling to a crescendo that seemed to throb through her. Max's hand slid caressingly over her shoulder, down her arm, his fingers lingering just inches from her right breast.

Ryan turned her head to look at him and caught just a glimpse of his smug smile.

She straightened abruptly in her seat, dislodging his hand.

Max immediately moved his arm, his expression innocently questioning. She focused her attention on the screen for the remainder of the movie, shaking her head when he offered her more popcorn.

By the time the film ended and the theater lights came back on, she had herself firmly under control.

Max insisted on walking her to her car, which she'd left in the parking garage behind the mall. "You're sure you wouldn't like to have coffee and dessert somewhere?" he asked for the third time since the movie had ended.

"No, thank you," she said, as she had the other times. "It's late and I have to work tomorrow."

Standing very close to her, he backed her against her car and gave her a smile so seductive that Ryan figured he must have started practicing it in the mirror the day he hit puberty. She didn't doubt that he'd been quite successful with it. It was all she could do to resist it herself.

"I really had a great time with you tonight," he said, his voice deep and sexy. "Thank you for agreeing to see me."

With an effort, she made her own smile bright and impersonal. "I had a nice time, too, Max," she said lightly. "The movie was amusing, and I needed a break."

He lifted a hand to stroke her cheek. She trembled at his touch, though she tried to hide her reaction.

She'd have bet her Christmas profits that he'd practiced this look, too. A look that tempted a woman to believe he found her beautiful. Desirable. Special.

"I want to see you again," he murmured, his mouth hovering mere inches above hers. So close she could feel his warm breath caressing her cheek, making her tingle in response.

Oh, yeah, he was good. Even knowing exactly what he was, she might have been as susceptible as the next woman, if he'd come along a year ago. Six months, even.

Okay, so maybe she'd been accused of being rigid and inflexible on occasion. Maybe she was. But her thirtieth birthday was inching closer and she didn't for a minute believe that Max was looking for a permanent relationship. A holiday fling was all he had in mind, and she simply didn't have time for such foolishness. Nor would she put her heart at risk with a man who'd undoubtedly broken more than his share of them.

"I'd better go," she said, sliding skillfully out of his loose embrace just as his mouth lowered toward hers. "Thanks again, Max. It's been fun."

He blinked. His expression would probably make her laugh when she thought about it later. Obviously, he wasn't accustomed to having women cut him short when he went into his turn-her-knees-to-jelly routine. "Uh—"

She opened her car door. "Good night, Max. Maybe I'll see you around sometime."

"But—when?" he demanded, trying to detain her.

She closed the door and smiled through the driver's-side window. "Good night," she called through the glass, deliberately ignoring his question.

She started the engine. He had to move back quickly

or she would have flattened his toes as she drove away from him.

She glanced into her rearview mirror. He was still standing where she'd left him, looking after her with obvious bewilderment. She smiled sadly.

He wasn't such a bad sort. A little vain, definitely cocky, but he was charming and probably a lot of fun to spend time with. At least until he grew bored and moved on.

As intriguing as he was, Max Monroe was no more husband-and-father material than…than the mall Santa was the real Santa Claus, Ryan told herself ruefully.

It was a shame, actually. Max Monroe was the first man who'd made her tremble in longer than she could remember.

LYNN STONE and part-time employee Cathy Patterson spent the first hour at work Sunday afternoon trying to get Ryan to tell them about her date with Max. She told them she'd had a nice time, advised them to see the film for themselves and informed them firmly that she had no plans to see Max in the future.

"Did he ask?" Lynn demanded, daring her to lie.

Ryan sighed. "He asked. I said no. There's no point in it, Lynn. He's just not my type."

"Lynn said he was gorgeous," Cathy said. "And that he had a killer smile."

"He is and he does," Ryan admitted. "But that's not enough reason for me to get involved with him."

"And why not?" Lynn challenged. "Do you really want to spend the entire holiday season alone?"

"I'm not alone. I have my father and my brother. And I *used* to have good friends," Ryan added pointedly.

As she had expected, Lynn ignored the subtle rebuke. "But as you said yourself, it's a couples' season. And you aren't even dating anyone. Wouldn't you at least like to have a date for New Year's Eve?"

"You," Ryan told her friend, "are making me crazy.

Would you stop with this Max thing? Couldn't you tell by looking at him that he's nothing but trouble? You know I would love to meet someone and fall deeply in love and get married and live happily ever after. But not with a guy like that. He's not the settling-down type."

"Okay," Lynn conceded. "So Max Monroe probably isn't destined to be your soul mate. But do you have to be alone all the time while you wait for Mr. Right to appear? Can't you just have fun with a guy occasionally? And even you have to admit that Max would probably be a lot of fun, especially if you don't expect too much from him to start with."

"From what Lynn's told me about him, I'd bet he'd be a *lot* of fun," Cathy seconded. "Loosen up, Ryan. Enjoy yourself for a change. Then, when the right guy does appear, you'll be ready to settle down and devote the rest of your life to raising kids and running that chain of doll shops you have in mind."

Ryan shook her head. She didn't see any reason to mention that she was ready for that now—more than ready.

She'd accomplished so many of the goals she'd set on her twentieth birthday. She'd seen Europe and Australia. She'd earned her degree, with honors. She'd started her own business and thus far was doing very well with it.

She had a great apartment, a lot of good friends, a loving and supportive family. All that was lacking was a life partner.

And no man she'd met so far had even come close to the ideal mate she had in mind. Including Max Monroe.

"Excuse me," she said to her co-workers. "I believe I see a customer in need of assistance. Several of them, as a matter of fact."

Finally taking the hint, Lynn and Cathy busied themselves in the shop. Ryan did the same.

IT WAS JUST BEFORE THREE when she spotted the little girl standing in front of the dark-haired doll. Ryan was surprised. She hadn't expected to see Kelsey at the mall for a third day in a row. She appeared to be alone this time; Pip was nowhere in sight.

Ryan moved toward the child. "Hello, Kelsey. This is a nice surprise."

Kelsey's rosy face lit up with her smile. "Hi, Ryan. I just came to visit the doll again."

"You're always welcome to stop in," Ryan answered. "Um—is your mother with you?"

Kelsey's smile faded. "No, ma'am. My mother's dead."

Ryan choked. "Oh, sweetheart, I'm sorry, I didn't know. Where—where's Pip?"

"He went to the park," Kelsey replied, carefully holding the dark-haired doll. "He wanted to see Max play football."

"Surely someone is here with you." Ryan couldn't believe that a tiny six-year-old was in a crowded shopping mall alone.

"Pip brought me," Kelsey volunteered. "He said for me to stay here until he comes to pick me up. He gave me a dollar," she added, digging in the pocket of her faded little jeans. She held up a well-used bill. "See? He said I could buy a cookie."

Genuinely concerned now, Ryan knelt in front of the little girl. "Kelsey—sweetie, surely there's someone who takes care of you. Someone besides Pip, I mean. Your father, maybe?"

Kelsey shook her head, her blue eyes huge and somber. "My daddy died, too. With my mommy. They were in a plane crash. Me and Pip live with Aunt Opal, but she's gone to California."

"Who is taking care of you while your aunt is away?" Ryan asked. Or, rather, who *should* be taking care of them? she wondered grimly.

"Mrs. Culpepper. She's our landlady."

"Does she know you're at the mall alone?"

Kelsey bit her lower lip. "Well…"

The child's expression was quite revealing.

Ryan thought of Pip, out on the streets alone. It was no more safe for him at the park than it was for Kelsey to be alone in a crowded mall.

Ryan wouldn't be able to put her mind at ease until she knew he was safe.

She sighed and straightened. "Lynn, I'm taking the rest of the afternoon off, okay? Will you and Cathy be okay without me?"

Lynn looked surprised, but nodded. "Of course we will. Is anything wrong?"

"No," she assured her. "There's just something I have to do." She turned to Kelsey. "Let's go find Pip, shall we?"

Kelsey looked indecisive. "I don't know. He told me to wait here."

Ryan gave the little girl a warm smile. "I don't think he'll mind if you're with me. I'll take full responsibility."

Kelsey nodded. "Okay." She kissed the doll's cool plastic cheek. "Bye, Annie," she said, carefully placing her back on the shelf.

"Annie?" Ryan repeated curiously.

Kelsey's head bobbed again. "I like that name, don't you?"

"Yes. It's a very nice name." Ryan held out her hand to the child. "Shall we go?"

Kelsey slipped her tiny fingers trustingly into Ryan's.

4

THE PARK WAS a big one, with acres and acres of rolling hills and partially cleared woods. Facilities included a golf course, several baseball fields, a public swimming pool, bike and hiking trails, playgrounds, pavilions and picnic tables—the city had gone all out to provide something for everyone. Ryan only hoped she'd be able to find one little boy in such a large place.

Fortunately, it wasn't peak season for park visitors. Driving her car slowly along the park roads, Ryan quickly spotted a group of men and women engaged in a rowdy game of touch football. She hoped it was Max's group and that Pip had also found them.

She parked in the nearest empty space. "Button your jacket, Kelsey, it's cool out," she said automatically.

Kelsey unsnapped her seat belt and fumbled with the buttons of her too-thin jacket. "Two of the buttons are gone," she said matter-of-factly. "I lost them."

"That's okay," Ryan assured her with a slight pang. "Button the rest of them."

She zipped her own heavier, lined jacket as she stepped out of her car. She was glad she'd worn pants instead of a skirt that day, having chosen another Christmas-patterned sweater with dark green slacks and comfortable brown loafers.

Kelsey met her at the front of the car, taking her hand as casually as though they'd known each other for ages. Wrapping her fingers warmly around the little girl's, Ryan led her toward the small crowd clustered in the park common.

She spotted Max almost immediately. Dressed in a gray sweatshirt and jeans, his blond hair blowing in the wind, he was running downfield, his arms outstretched to catch a pass. She felt her heart jump and told herself she was here only to find Pip, not to see Max again. No matter how good he looked to her.

Max saw Ryan just as the quarterback released the football. He dropped his arms and stumbled. The ball hit him squarely in the back, to the groaning dismay of his team and the delight of the opposing players, who hooted derisively.

Grinning, Max called for time out and loped toward Ryan. "Hi! It's great to see you here. I didn't expect…" He paused when he noticed the child with her. "Oh. Hello, Kelsey."

The little girl dimpled, delighted at the greeting. "Hi."

Max looked questioningly at Ryan.

"Have you seen Pip?" Ryan asked him. "He said he was coming here to watch you play."

"I haven't seen him."

Ryan winced. "Oh, no."

Kelsey looked up with wide eyes. "Do you think Pip got lost?" she asked in a small voice.

"What's going on?" Max inquired.

"Hey, Max—are you playing or what?" someone shouted impatiently.

He waved a hand. "Put someone in for me," he called back. "Something's come up."

"Pip dropped Kelsey off at the mall and headed here," Ryan explained, looking around carefully in search of one sandy-haired little boy. "He was on foot and alone."

Max frowned. "Where are their parents? Do they know the kids are out on their own?"

In a low voice, Ryan quickly told him the situation Kelsey had outlined for her.

By the time she finished, Max looked grim. "We'd better find him," he said. "I'll get some of my friends to help us look."

Ryan nodded. "We'll split up. I'll go that way and you and your friends can—"

"Kelsey! Hey, what are you doing here?"

The call from behind made them both whirl around quickly. With almost overwhelming relief, Ryan saw Pip running toward them, waving. Like Kelsey, he wore a jacket that was too thin for the weather, and jeans split at the knees. His nose and cheeks were reddened from the cold air.

"Pip!" Ryan reached out to touch him, just to reassure herself he was unharmed. "You worried us," she said. "You really shouldn't be out on the streets alone. It isn't safe."

The boy looked surprised. "I can take care of myself," he assured her earnestly.

Hesitant to hurt his feelings, Ryan nodded. "I know you can, but—"

"She's right, you know, pal," Max said. "The park isn't a very safe place for a kid on his own. And the mall isn't a safe place for little girls to be alone, either," he added.

Pip's face fell. "I guess I shouldn't have left Kelsey by herself," he admitted. "But she wanted to look at the dolls and I wanted to watch your football game. I saw part of it, but I had to go to the rest room. You're a good player, Max."

"I didn't see you watching."

"I didn't want to distract you," Pip replied.

"Everything okay here, Max?" a black man with kind eyes asked from nearby.

Max nodded. "Count me out for the rest of the game, will you, Stan?"

Looking speculatively at Ryan and the children, his friend nodded. "Yeah, sure."

Kelsey tugged at Ryan's hand. "There's the playground," she said, pointing across the park. "I want to go swing."

"C'mon, Kelsey. I'll take you to the swings," Pip said, automatically falling back into the authority role with her.

"Wait," Ryan said quickly, tightening her fingers around Kelsey's hand. She didn't care how long Pip had been taking care of his little sister, she wasn't letting these children out of her sight again until there was an adult to supervise them. "Won't Mrs. Culpepper be wondering where you are?"

Pip seemed startled that Ryan knew the name. He looked narrowly at his sister. "Mrs. C. doesn't expect us home until five," he explained. He tapped his Batman watch. "We've got about an hour before we have to start walking home."

Ryan bit her tongue to keep from expressing her opinion of a woman who allowed two children to roam the streets unsupervised. "Do you mind if I come with you to the playground?" she asked instead. "I'd like to watch you play."

"That sounds like fun!" Kelsey bounced in excitement. "Will you come, too, Max?"

"Sure. Just let me get my stuff."

Ryan and the children remained where they were while Max ran over to a bench piled with coats and other paraphernalia.

Ryan thought maybe she'd talk to him about the children while the kids played on the playground equipment. Not that she expected him to be much help, but she felt the need to discuss the situation with another adult before she decided what to do.

Even if the only available adult happened to be Max Monroe.

Before Max rejoined them, an attractive black woman with two small children in tow approached Ryan. "Do you know if the game's almost over?" she asked. "I'm here to pick up my husband."

"No, I'm sorry, I don't know how long they'll be."

The woman looked at Ryan in curiosity. "I'm Stan's wife, Gayle. Are you Ben's wife?"

"No." She seemed to expect more of an explanation, so Ryan cleared her throat. "I'm with Max. Sort of."

"Max Monroe?" Gayle looked over to the bench, where Max was talking to another man as he donned a denim jacket. "He and my Stan have been friends for years."

Ryan wasn't sure what to say. She settled for a smile.

"I don't know Max very well myself," Gayle admitted. "But I love his books."

"His…books?"

Gayle nodded. "M. L. Monroe is one of my favorite authors. I just wish he would write more. Stan says—"

Max joined them then. "Hi, Gayle. Here to collect Stan?"

"Yes."

"He should be finished soon. The game's almost over."

Gayle smiled, looking at Max a bit shyly. "Thanks."

Kelsey shuffled her feet. "Are you ready now, Max?"

He smiled. "Yes, I'm ready. See you around, Gayle."

They'd taken only a few steps toward the playground when they were detained yet again, this time by a bubbly blonde in a skintight, cropped sweater and her similarly dressed young friend. After a moment, Ryan recognized the blonde: Brittany, who worked at the ice-cream parlor across the mall from Beautiful Babies.

"Max!" Brittany crooned. "I was hoping you'd still be here. This is my friend, Marti."

"Hi. Brittany, isn't it?"

She giggled and nodded. "Is the game over?" she asked, looking sideways at Ryan and the children.

"No, it's still on. Why don't you and your friend go join in?"

Brittany bit her full lower lip. "But I thought you said you would be playing."

"I'm through. Go on over, though. It's an open game. You and Marti will be welcome."

Brittany stuck out her lip in a pout. "But—"

Two grinning young men skidded to a stop a few feet

away. "Hi," they said, staring wide-eyed at Brittany and Marti. "Are you here for the game? We could introduce you."

Ryan hadn't missed Max's subtle signal to call the young men over. Though Brittany pouted a bit, she allowed herself to be led away and was giggling again before a full minute had passed.

Ryan gave Max a cool glance. "Why don't you stay with your friends? I'll watch the children and make sure they get home."

Kelsey looked disappointed. "But Max said he wanted to come with us."

"And I do," he assured her. "Let's go before someone stops us again."

When they reached the playground, Kelsey ran straight to the swings. Max helped her onto one and then stood behind her to give her a push. Her chubby legs pumped the air, her hair flying out behind her as she soared, squealing and laughing. Pip stood nearby with a smile and a protective expression.

Taking a seat on a nearby bench, Ryan watched pensively, thinking that Pip hardly seemed like a child himself. He was much too serious for a boy his age. Didn't he ever act silly, the way most pre-adolescent boys behaved?

Catching his eye, she pointed to a tower slide behind the swings. "That looks like fun," she said. "Why don't you try it?"

Pip took one more look at Kelsey, as though making sure she was having a good time, and then he nodded and ran over to agilely climb the eight-foot tower. Ryan noted in satisfaction that he was grinning as he shot down the winding tube of aluminum on the seat of his faded jeans. Hitting the ground on both feet, he immediately started climbing again.

Ryan's attention turned back to Kelsey, but before long she found herself staring at Max. He looked particularly attractive at play, his dark gold hair tumbled around his wind-reddened cheeks, his blue-gray eyes gleaming, his crooked smile flashing.

She thought of what she'd learned about him only minutes earlier.

M. L. Monroe. She'd had no idea that Max was the popular writer, author of a fast-paced series starring a foot-loose adventurer who answered only to the name of Montana.

She'd read a couple of the books herself, though her brother Nick was the true fan. Nick had raved about the series on more than one occasion, even mentioning that there was a potential movie deal in the works.

Ryan couldn't help wondering how much of himself Max wrote into his hero.

Montana was a man who played at life the way some people played at cards. The restless type, always off in search of a new challenge. Never staying in any place long enough to set down even the most shallow of roots.

A heartbreaker.

She couldn't really say she was surprised that the gorgeous and cocky Max Monroe had created the character.

Leaving Kelsey to play with Pip, Max joined Ryan on the bench. "Kelsey told me I was the best swinger she'd ever met."

Ryan didn't share his obvious amusement. "I'm sure she's right," she said coolly.

He cleared his throat. "Er, about Brittany…"

"I have to decide what to do about the children," she said, ignoring him. "It's obvious that they aren't being properly cared for. It's only a matter of time before one of them is hurt or—or worse."

"What, exactly, did Kelsey tell you?"

"That her parents are dead. That she and Pip live with her aunt Opal, but her aunt is away, leaving them in the care of their landlady, a Mrs. Culpepper. On the way over here, I asked her to tell me more about Mrs. Culpepper. She was very vague. She said only that the woman doesn't seem to like children very much. It didn't sound as though they are being physically abused, but they are most definitely being neglected."

"Maybe their aunt has no idea what sort of woman she's left them with. Does Kelsey know how to reach her?"

Ryan shook her head. "She said she doesn't know where her aunt is. Only that she said she had to get away from work and kids for a while. Apparently, that was the last thing she said to them as she left them with the landlady."

"Damn." Max looked grimly at the two children, watching as Pip climbed the slide tower behind Kelsey, protecting her with outstretched arms. "That boy's something else, isn't he? I've never met a kid quite like him."

"I was just thinking that he's much too serious for a child his age. He takes his responsibilities very much to heart."

"They seem to have bonded very quickly with you."

Ryan bit her lip. "I know. And I'm a total stranger to them. What do you think I should do?"

"Me?" Max asked, looking startled. "Hell, I don't know. This isn't really my area of expertise."

She bit her tongue. "Maybe I should call my brother, Nick," she murmured, almost to herself.

"Why?"

"He's an attorney. He'd be more likely to know the legal procedures for making sure children are being properly cared for."

"He'll probably suggest calling child-welfare services. Pip and Kelsey will probably be taken from the landlady and put into foster care until their aunt is found."

Ryan frowned. "You really think so?"

"What else could anyone do?" he asked logically.

"I've heard some real horror stories about foster care."

"I'm sure most foster homes are decent places." Max sounded as though he meant to be reassuring. "You know how the media tends to focus only on the worst of the bunch."

"You don't suppose anyone would try to split them up, do you? Pip and Kelsey would be miserable if they weren't together. Even I can see that, after spending very little time with them."

Now Max was frowning. "I don't know," he admitted. "I hadn't thought of that. Surely they'd keep them together."

But he didn't sound as confident as Ryan would have liked.

"I'm going to take them home and meet Mrs. Culpepper," Ryan said in sudden decision. "Maybe she isn't as bad as we think. Maybe she doesn't know the children have been out alone so much. Maybe she thinks they're at a friend's house or something."

"Maybe," Max said, still sounding doubtful.

Ryan didn't really believe it, either, but she had to find out for herself. She glanced at her watch. "It's almost four-thirty. I should probably take them home soon."

"I'll come with you."

Startled by the offer, she looked at Max warily. "Why?"

"Now you've got me concerned about them," he admitted. "They're cute kids. I'd hate to see something happen to them. Besides," he added with a winning smile, "I need a ride myself. One of my buddies picked me up this afternoon and he left the park while we've been watching the kids play."

Ryan sighed.

"You don't mind, do you, Ryan?"

There didn't seem to be much she could say. After all, she had sort of dragged him into this situation—though only because Pip had decided he wanted to watch Max play football. "I guess not."

Max didn't comment on her obvious lack of enthusiasm. He simply nodded and rose to his feet. "Maybe we should go. It's getting colder and that little jacket Kelsey has on isn't very warm. Her lips are starting to turn blue."

If he was deliberately trying to disarm her, he succeeded. Ryan couldn't help but be a bit touched by his concern for little Kelsey—assuming, of course, it wasn't just an act for her benefit.

She motioned to the children.

Obediently, they raced up to her. Kelsey wrapped an arm trustingly around Max's legs, making his eyes widen in surprise, though he awkwardly patted her shoulder as she smiled up at him. "What's up?" she asked.

Ryan smiled at the phrasing. "It's time to go," she said. "You said Mrs. Culpepper expects you by five."

Pip looked at his own watch. "Yeah, it's time," he agreed. He held out his hand to his sister. "C'mon, Kelsey, we better hurry."

Ryan placed a hand on Pip's shoulder. "I'll drive you."

Pip looked hesitant. "That's okay, Ryan," he said. "We don't live far from here. We can walk."

"I'd really like to drive you." She chose her words carefully, not wanting to hurt the boy's pride. "It's getting colder, and as Max just pointed out, Kelsey's lips are turning blue. We wouldn't want her to catch cold, would we?"

She'd hit on the one argument Pip couldn't refute. He looked a bit torn for a moment, then nodded shyly. "Okay. Thanks."

THE APARTMENT BUILDING Pip directed Ryan to was old and rundown, only a few blocks from the mall and the park, in a neighborhood Ryan always carefully avoided after dark. She didn't at all like the thought of the children wandering these streets alone. She was more determined than ever to talk to their caretaker.

As Pip and Kelsey struggled out of their seat belts, Ryan unsnapped hers and reached for the door handle. "I'll walk you in," she said casually.

Pip's eyes widened. "That's okay," he said a bit too quickly. "You don't have to do that."

"I would like to," Ryan replied. "I want to meet your landlady."

Pip chewed his bottom lip. "She won't like it if she thinks me and Kelsey have been any trouble."

Ryan held on to her smile with an effort. "I'll make sure she knows you aren't any trouble."

Max had already opened his door. "So will I."

Kelsey climbed out of the car without hesitation. Pip seemed a bit more reluctant, but he didn't try any further protests.

The entry hall was dim and stale smelling. Ryan wrinkled her nose, then immediately smoothed her expression, not wanting the children to see her distaste for their home.

"This is our 'partment," Kelsey said, pointing to the first door on the right. "Mrs. Culpepper lives in that one down there."

"You have been staying with her, haven't you?" Ryan asked, curious about the child's wording.

Kelsey shook her head. "We sleep at our place. Mrs. C. gives us our dinner and makes sure we get up for school, but we aren't 'xactly staying with her."

Appalled, Ryan looked at Max. This was even worse than she'd thought. The children were basically living alone. How could their aunt have left them under these conditions?

Max's expression reflected her own dismay. "I'd like to meet this 'Mrs. C.,'" he murmured.

"So would I," Ryan said grimly.

Pip still looked nervous. He twisted his thin little hands in front of him. "She isn't going to like it that we talked to strangers."

"We won't tell her we're strangers. We'll tell her we're old friends, come to check on you while your aunt's away," Max assured him. "That sounds perfectly reasonable, doesn't it?"

Pip nodded hesitantly.

Ryan didn't approve of teaching the children to lie, but she could see that Max's tale had merit. It would keep the children out of trouble with their baby-sitter and give her and Max an excuse to make sure they were being well cared for.

"Why don't you and Kelsey go inside your apartment and wash up?" she suggested. "Max and I will visit with Mrs. Culpepper for a few minutes. We'll let you know when we're leaving."

"You won't go without saying goodbye?" Kelsey asked, looking a bit anxious now.

"Of course not," Ryan assured her with a gentle smile. On impulse, she smoothed the little girl's hair, noting how cool Kelsey's skin felt. "Go into your apartment now, sweetie," she urged. "You need to get warm again."

Ryan waited until the children closed their door behind them. Then she turned to Max, her fists clenched. "Let's go talk to this landlady," she said through gritted teeth. "I have a few things to say to her."

Max reached out and caught her arm. "Chill out, Ryan," he suggested. "You won't help the kids if you make their landlady angry with them."

Aware that he was right, she drew a calming breath. "It makes me furious that no one seems to care about their safety."

"We don't know that yet," he reminded her. "Not for certain."

She only looked at him.

He made a sheepish face. "Okay, they're obviously being neglected," he conceded. "And it makes me mad, too. But we have to keep in mind that it isn't really our business."

"Child abuse is everyone's business, Max. It's thinking like yours that allows the injustices to continue. You know the saying—the only thing necessary for the triumph of evil is for good men, or women, in this case, to do nothing."

"Edmund Burke," Max commented. "But don't over-react, Ryan. You said yourself that the children don't seem to have been abused. Neglected, certainly, but—"

"Is there really that much difference?" she asked him quietly.

He fell silent. And then he shrugged. "Let's go talk to the landlady, shall we?"

She nodded and headed determinedly for the door the children had indicated.

5

THE FIRST THING Ryan noticed about the woman who opened the door was that she smelled like cheap beer and even cheaper perfume. She was heavyset, dour faced, badly permed and carelessly dressed.

She looked at Ryan and Max in the hallway and immediately grew defensive. "What do you want?" she asked. "I know you ain't interested in an apartment here."

Ryan forced a small smile. "Mrs. Culpepper?"

The woman eyed her suspiciously. "Yeah?"

"My name is Ryan Clark. This is my friend, Max Monroe. May we talk with you for a moment?"

"What about?" the woman demanded, without moving from where she blocked the doorway.

"It's about Pip and Kelsey." Ryan suddenly realized that she didn't know the children's last name. She hoped she would be able to bluff her way past that omission.

"What about them? Have they been causin' you any trouble? If so, I'll—"

"They haven't caused us any trouble," Max assured her, stepping forward with one of his patented smiles. "Please forgive us for disturbing you this afternoon. We're friends of the children's aunt Opal, and we promised her we'd check on them from time to time while she was away."

Some of the suspicion left the woman's face—proving that even this old battle-ax wasn't entirely immune to Max Monroe's charm, Ryan thought resignedly.

"You're friends of Opal's?" Mrs. Culpepper asked, looking surprised. "I never seen you around here before."

"No," Max agreed without explanation. "We understand she asked you to watch out for her niece and nephew while she was on her vacation."

"Yeah. And I been doing it, too," the woman said defensively. "Feed 'em dinner every night. Make sure they get up for school every morning. Pip takes pretty good care of the little girl, so they don't need me hanging around every minute, but I've kept a close eye on 'em."

Ryan bit her tongue.

Max's smile never wavered. "They're good kids," he said.

"They're okay. But I raised my own kids and I don't want to take on any more. Have you heard from that aunt of theirs?"

"You mean you haven't heard from her?" Ryan asked, startled.

Mrs. Culpepper shook her head. "Not since she left. She said she'd call me and let me know when she was getting back, but I haven't heard nothing from her in more than two weeks. That ain't like her."

"I didn't realize she'd been gone that long," Max said thoughtfully.

"Yeah. Said she had her a new beau and they was going to California to look for jobs there. Said she'd send for the kids as soon as she had a place. One of 'em, anyway."

"One of them?" Ryan repeated, frowning.

Mrs. Culpepper nodded her fuzzy head. "She said the two of 'em was getting to be too much for her to manage. Kids are expensive, you know. Soon as she finds a place, she's taking one of them and sending the other up East to be with her sister. They've been arguing over which one gets the girl."

Max rested a hand on Ryan's shoulder when she would have burst out in protest of the plan to separate Pip and his sister. "Do you happen to have a number for Opal's sister?" he inquired. "Perhaps she can tell us how we might reach Opal."

"You think I haven't already tried the number I had for her? It's been disconnected. I called information, and there ain't no listing for an Essie Smith."

Ryan couldn't stay silent any longer. "But what were you supposed to do in case of an emergency?"

"There better not be any emergencies," the woman said with a scowl. "If I don't hear from Opal in a couple of days, I'm calling child welfare to come get the kids. I don't like doin' it, but I got no other choice. The rent runs out at the end of this month and I can't be responsible for someone else's kids."

"You don't think she's abandoned them, do you?" Ryan asked worriedly, tensing at the woman's mention of child welfare.

"I don't know," Mrs. Culpepper replied wearily. "Wouldn't be the first time it happened 'round here."

"How does Opal seem to feel about the children?" Max asked. "Is she fond of them?"

Mrs. Culpepper frowned. "Don't you know?"

He gave her another of his winsome smiles. "I'd just like your opinion," he said.

She shrugged. "She's a young woman, not forty yet. And she likes men, you know? Not many of 'em are interested in a woman with two kids around. Her sister's a couple years younger, been married twice and lookin' for number three. Neither of them planned on raising their brother's kids." *And who could blame them?* her expression seemed to ask.

"Why didn't they give them up for adoption?" Ryan mused aloud.

The woman shook her head. "I guess they thought they had an obligation to 'em or something. And then there was the kids' Social Security checks...."

Ryan was appalled that the children's meager monthly checks could be the only reason their aunt had taken them in. Mrs. Culpepper seemed to accept it as a matter of fact. Ryan wondered just how much the woman had been paid to watch out for Pip and Kelsey these two weeks.

"This is terrible," she whispered.

A world of unpleasant experience was in the older woman's faded eyes. "Lady, compared to some of 'em, these kids got it good." She shook her head, as though shaking off ugly memories. "Look, is there anything else you was wanting to ask? I got a stew on the stove for the kids' dinner and I got to get back to it."

"There isn't anything else for now," Max said when Ryan would have spoken. "You've been very patient, Mrs. Culpepper. Thank you."

The woman nodded. "Send the kids on down if you see 'em on your way out."

"We'll do that," Max assured her. He started to pull Ryan away.

She resisted. "Mrs. Culpepper," she said, just as the other woman began to close the door. The landlady paused, her expression impatient.

Ryan dug into the outside pocket of her purse and pulled out a business card. She hastily scribbled her home number on the back.

"I can be reached at one of these two numbers if you or the children need me," she said, pressing the card into the woman's work-worn hand. "If you hear from their aunt, I would appreciate it if you would give me a call. And, please, promise me that you won't call the welfare services without calling me first."

The woman sighed heavily. "All right. But at the end of the month, they have to go. That's only four more days."

"I know. And I promise you, I'll make arrangements for them if you don't hear from their aunt by then," Ryan vowed impulsively. "Just call me, okay?"

The woman tucked the card inside the pocket of her too-tight knit slacks. "I'll call you."

"Thank you."

"Send the kids down for supper. It's ready for 'em." The landlady closed the door without giving Ryan another chance to detain her.

Ryan rubbed her temples with both hands. "Oh, dear," she muttered. "What a mess."

Max rested a hand on her shoulder. "Ryan, are you really sure you should be getting involved with this? I mean, you don't know these people. You have no authority to interfere. You could be getting into all sorts of trouble—legal trouble, for that matter."

Ryan dropped her hands and rounded on him, her chin high, her temper blazing. "Look," she said flatly. "For that matter, I don't really know *you*. If you don't want to get involved, fine. Leave. I can't. Those children, for whatever reason, have decided they can trust me, and I'm not going to just walk away from them now that I know they might be in trouble. But no one's expecting you to put yourself out for them. If you hurry, maybe you can get back to the park before Brittany and Marti leave."

Max's eyes narrowed. For the first time in her presence, he lost that easygoing, isn't-this-fun expression—and Ryan realized that he could look just a bit intimidating when he tried.

She lifted her chin higher, refusing to flinch.

"I felt that I had the responsibility to point out the hazards to you," he said, his voice clipped. "Now that I have, I think we should go tell the children good-night. We promised we wouldn't leave without letting them know."

"I didn't intend to."

He nodded curtly. "Fine. Let's go."

RYAN HATED TO LEAVE the children alone, knowing they would be spending the night in the apartment without an adult. "Why don't you ask Mrs. Culpepper if you can stay with her tonight?" she suggested after she delivered the message that their dinner was waiting for them.

"Why?" Pip asked curiously.

"Wouldn't you feel safer?" she asked.

He shrugged. "We keep the doors and windows locked. And Mrs. C. checks on us at bedtime and gets us up in the mornings. We're safe enough."

She hated it—truly hated it—but Max was right in one respect. Ryan had no authority to do anything more, unless she was prepared to contact the authorities. Which she wasn't, yet. Not without talking to her brother first.

"Is there a telephone here?" she asked them, looking around the surprisingly clean, but pitifully inadequate two-bedroom apartment in which they lived.

Pip shook his head. "Aunt Opal can't afford one," he admitted. "We can use Mrs. C.'s sometimes."

"She has my number," Ryan said, pulling out another card and writing her home number on the back. "You keep this, Pip. If you need me—anytime at all—you call me, okay?"

"Okay. Can we come back to see you at the mall?" Both Pip and Kelsey looked at her beseechingly.

Ryan glanced helplessly at Max. He waited silently to hear her answer.

"I suppose so," she said to the children after a moment, thinking that it was only a few blocks from their school to the mall. "But, please, be careful, Pip. You really shouldn't be out on the streets alone."

"We'll be careful," he assured her.

Kelsey threw her arms around Ryan's waist. "'Bye, Ryan," she said, trustingly lifting her little face.

Swallowing a huge lump in her throat, Ryan leaned over to kiss her soft cheek. "'Bye, sweetie. See you soon, okay?"

Max solemnly shook Pip's hand, "Take care of your little sister."

"I always have," Pip replied, sounding heartbreakingly matter-of-fact about it. "'Bye, Max. See you, Ryan."

Leaving them there was the hardest thing Ryan had ever done.

"I CAN'T BELIEVE IT. I just can't believe the way those children are being raised. Doesn't anyone care that anything could happen to them while they're alone on the streets— or in their own apartment, for that matter? It's just a miracle that nothing has happened yet. And as for this insane idea to separate them, hasn't anyone noticed how close they are? How much they depend on each other? It would devastate them if they—"

"Ryan," Max interrupted gently. "Breathe."

She took a short, choppy breath, her hands so tight on the steering wheel that her knuckles ached.

"Where do you live, anyway?" she asked, suddenly aware that she'd been driving aimlessly ever since leaving the children's apartment building fifteen minutes earlier.

"On the other side of town. How about if we stop and get a hamburger or something on the way?"

She started to decline.

He forestalled her by saying, "We could talk about the children, maybe come up with some ideas."

She slanted him a skeptical look. Would he actually use the children as an excuse to get her to have dinner with him? Or was that incredibly egotistical of her?

She nodded. "All right—though I'm not sure what we could do for them without knowing a bit more about their situation."

"True," he agreed. "But maybe we'll think of something. And besides," he added, "I'm starving. Even Mrs. Culpepper's beef stew smelled inviting."

"I don't know how you could smell it over her perfume," Ryan grumbled.

Max touched her arm. "The children will be all right for tonight," he assured her. "Try to relax, okay?"

"I'll try," she said with a sigh. "But it isn't easy. I really hated leaving them, Max."

"I know you did. You're a very caring person, Ryan Clark. Be careful that soft heart of yours doesn't get you into trouble someday."

She couldn't help wondering if his warning had to do with something other than the children.

MAX WATCHED RYAN as they settled into a fast-food-restaurant booth with their food. He had ordered a chicken club sandwich, large fries and a jug-size soft drink; Ryan settled for a salad, baked potato—hold the sour cream—and a diet soda.

She seemed to be the weight-conscious type, he thought as he took a bite of his sandwich. Surreptitiously eyeing her figure, he couldn't imagine why she worried about it. She looked darned near perfect to him.

Her thoughts obviously far away, Ryan toyed with her food. "What should we do?" she asked finally.

Realizing that she was still concentrating on the children, Max gave a mental sigh and shook off the thoughts that would only get him into trouble with her. She'd made it clear enough that she wasn't exactly ready to fall into his arms. No matter how eager he was for her to do so.

If Ryan wanted to talk about the kids, they'd talk about the kids. At least she was talking to him again. When they'd parted the night before, he hadn't been at all sure he'd have this chance again. He'd gone to bed alone last night, wondering if he was losing his touch.

"The logical answer would be to report the situation to the proper authorities," he said, knowing as he spoke that she wouldn't like the suggestion. "Tell them what we've observed, suggest that they look into the situation."

He was right about her reaction. Her eyes darkened,

and that intriguingly dimpled chin of hers lifted stubbornly. "Do you know what would happen to the children if we did that?"

"Foster care, most likely. If there was evidence to indicate that they've been abandoned, they would become wards of the state."

Ryan shuddered. "That sounds awful."

"It's a system designed to protect children," Max commented. "To give them a safe home and close supervision."

Ryan frowned. "But do we really have the right to interfere in that way? What if they *haven't* been abandoned? What if their aunt really does love them and wants the best for them? What if she believes Mrs. Culpepper is watching them closely?"

"There is that possibility," he agreed, though he didn't particularly believe it. If the aunt had been all that concerned about the kids, she wouldn't have left them under these conditions.

"If only we could find at least one of their aunts." Ryan had asked the children for their relatives' names before she'd left. Opal Coleman—same surname as the kids'—was the one who'd taken off for California two weeks ago. Her sister, Essie Smith, lived in Boston, according to Pip, though he'd had no specific address to give them.

"Mrs. Culpepper said she couldn't find a listing for Essie Smith," Ryan mused, as though thinking aloud. "I wonder how I could track her down without a phone number."

Max was wondering how he could get Ryan's full attention. She hadn't really looked at him since she'd interrupted his football game. Her attention was all for the orphaned siblings.

Studying her across the table, he felt that now-familiar tug of attraction. He wondered what it was about her that he found so appealing. Sure, she was pretty, but he'd known more-beautiful women. She had a nice smile and a great body, but so did plenty of others.

She'd certainly given him little encouragement. Though there had been times when she'd looked at him with what he would have sworn was an interest similar to his own, she always retreated before he could follow up on her signals. He didn't know what he'd done to make her cut him off so rapidly last night after the movie, and he'd begun to wonder if she'd ever let him get close enough again to find out.

What he needed was a reason to spend time with her, to find out what it was about him that spooked her. A chance to convince her that they could have fun together if she would just loosen up and give him the opportunity to show her a good time.

It had been several months since he'd been involved with anyone, even superficially. Ryan was the first woman who'd really interested him in quite a while. He suspected that they could have a great time together, at least until the excitement ended. And it always ended.

If only he could think of some way to convince her to give him a chance…

"I wonder if my brother could help contact their aunts," Ryan said, still concentrating on the children.

Max lifted his head as an idea occurred to him—a way to kill two birds with one stone, so to speak. He could do something to help those cute kids and give Ryan a reason to stay in contact with him at the same time.

"I have a friend who could possibly help us out," he said as he reached for his drink, his expression deliberately casual. "Her name's Juliana West."

Ryan looked cautiously intrigued. "What can your friend do for us?"

Pleased that he had her attention now, Max explained. "She's a former police officer turned private investigator. It's possible that she can get us something to go on. I'll give her these names, see what she can find out about them. In the meantime, you can stay in touch with Mrs. Culpepper and make sure the children are being properly cared for. I'll call you to check on them."

"But their rent runs out in four days. What if your friend hasn't located their aunts by then?"

"At that point we can assume that the children *have* been abandoned, either by design or some sort of accident. We'd have no alternative then but to contact the authorities. If we don't, their landlady certainly will."

Ryan nodded reluctantly. "I suppose you're right. Someone has to make sure the children aren't turned out on the street."

"You're sure you want to pursue it in this way? You don't think you should contact the authorities now?"

Ryan hesitated only a moment before shaking her head. "I want to wait. At least another day or two. As you said, we can monitor the children through Mrs. Culpepper for now. To be honest, I'm tempted to just take them home with me until we find out something about their aunts."

"And risk a kidnapping charge?" Max asked bluntly, unable to believe she'd actually consider such a step.

She didn't even know the kids, when it came right down to it. Cute as they were, how could she consider taking them in? She was young and single; she probably knew little more about taking care of a couple of kids than Max himself did. "You have no authorization for that, Ryan."

She sighed. "I know. It's just…"

"You're worried about them," he said understandingly. "And rightly so. So let's do what we can for them—legally."

He felt the faintest twinge of conscience, but he ignored it. Okay, so maybe he *was* using the children to get closer to Ryan. In the long run, both of them only wanted the best for the tots. He'd have Juliana look for their aunts, and if that failed, then he'd convince Ryan to turn the kids over to the proper authorities. Someone would take care of them.

Ryan thought about it a moment, then nodded. "All

right. I'll call Mrs. Culpepper to make sure the children are supervised after school tomorrow. You'll let me know as soon as your friend finds something, won't you?"

"Of course." He smiled winningly. "Now, since we've gotten ourselves caught up in a common problem, why don't you tell me more about yourself, Ryan Clark."

He figured it was well past time to get the conversation back to personal matters.

Ryan swallowed a mouthful of her salad and looked at him questioningly, obviously caught off guard by the sudden change of topic. "What do you want to know?"

"Are you from this area originally? What's your family like? Why did you decide to open your doll shop and what do you want to accomplish with it?"

Is your skin as soft as it looks? Your hair as silky? Does that pouty mouth taste as good as I think it would? When—if ever—will I have the chance to find out?

"You certainly ask a lot of questions," she said, unaware of the ones he'd left unspoken.

He only smiled and waited for her to provide some answers.

She speared a cherry tomato with her plastic fork. He could tell that she had to make an effort to take her mind off the children and answer him. "I am from this area. I have one brother—Nick, the attorney. My mother died several years ago, but my father still lives nearby. He's a retired attorney. Nick took over his practice a few years ago.

"I opened my shop because it's always been my goal to be self-employed and because I love dolls. I hope to own a small chain of Beautiful Babies stores eventually. In the meantime, I'm offering doll-making classes starting in the spring, and I hope to expand my current inventory to include more doll clothing and accessories, perhaps a select line of stuffed animals."

"It sounds as though you have your future all mapped out," Max commented.

"I have since I graduated from high school when I was twenty," she agreed after swallowing the tomato.

It took a moment for Max to realize what she'd said. "You were twenty when you finished high school?"

She nodded casually. "I was in a car accident three months into my junior year. It took over a year for me to fully recover from my injuries. I could have finished with a tutor, but I didn't want to miss out on the experience of having a senior year, so I went back to school as soon as I was physically able."

"And then what?" he asked, intrigued by the determination he heard in her tale.

"I spent the next two years traveling and working abroad. The Philippines. New Guinea. The Fiji Islands. Europe."

"You've been to Fiji?" Max was genuinely surprised. He would have bet good money that Ryan Clark was a sheltered, pampered young woman who'd rarely been more than a hundred miles from her family home.

Obviously, he would have been wrong.

She smiled at his expression. "Yes, I've been to Fiji. It's lovely there."

He was growing more fascinated by her with every revelation. "And then what did you do?"

"While I was in Europe, my mother passed away," she continued, a trace of grief deepening her voice. "I came home to spend more time with my father. I enrolled in the local university and earned a degree in business. I worked for a large toy-store chain for a couple of years while I prepared to open Beautiful Babies, which I did six months ago. I've already told you the rest of my career plans."

"You've accomplished quite a bit in twenty-eight years."

Her eyes were shuttered. "I had my reasons."

He would have liked to ask what those reasons were. Something told him she didn't want him to—and wouldn't answer if he did.

She didn't give him a chance to find out. "What about *you*? You aren't exactly what I'd expected of the famous M. L. Monroe."

Again she'd managed to surprise him. "How did you know?"

"Your friend Gayle mentioned it at the park earlier. She said you were one of her favorite writers. My brother's quite a fan of yours, as well. I'll have to tell him I've met you."

"I, er..." He was never quite comfortable when someone addressed him as M.L. the writer, rather than Max the person. Writing had been something he'd stumbled into almost by accident. It had given him financial security and the freedom to set his own working hours, to a great extent.

The fame was something he could have done without.

"What do you mean I'm not what you expected?" he asked.

"Nick said your books are bestsellers and there's even a movie deal pending. You're quite famous, and yet you've spent most of the past week hanging out at the mall or playing touch football at the park. I would have expected the creator of the fast-living Montana to lead a more adventurous existence."

Max was taken aback. Was *that* the way she'd read him? A lot of people would be surprised to hear her accuse him of leading a boring life. Especially those concerned friends and family members who'd often wondered aloud if he risked his life so regularly because he secretly placed too little value on it.

He lifted his chin in an arrogant way that those others would have instantly recognized. "And if I told you that I've been taking a few months off to write and mentally recharge before moving on again? That I've climbed some of the highest peaks in the world? That I've sailed in two international races? That I've played polo with a prince and gone deep-sea diving with a famous news-magazine anchor? That I've jumped out of planes and off mountains, raced cars, bicycles and motorcycles, tried my hand at rodeo, downhill skiing and bungee jumping?"

It was her turn to look startled. "*Have* you done all that?"

"Yes."

And more, he could have added. And still there was an empty feeling inside him, as though something was still out there waiting for him, something he'd been looking for most of his life and hadn't yet found, some as-yet-undiscovered adventure he needed to experience before he could feel satisfied.

Now it was Ryan who looked taken aback. She bit her lip and sighed. Max wondered why she looked so resigned when she smiled faintly and said, "Then I take back what I suggested about your life being staid. Why haven't I seen you in the society pages hobnobbing with the addictedly adventurous?"

He shrugged. "I'm not particularly photogenic."

She looked at him with a wry expression. "Yeah," she muttered. "Right."

He finished his sandwich, seeing no need to tell her how valuable his privacy was to him. About the freedom he found in relative anonymity, in having few expectations to live up to, no responsibilities to tie him down, nothing to keep him from picking up at a moment's notice and chasing his latest whim.

He was living a life most men only dreamed of. And if there were times when it didn't seem enough—well, that was only because he hadn't yet experienced everything out there.

Fiji, for example. He'd never been to Fiji.

"What about your family? Are they living in this area?" Ryan asked.

"There's my mother and my sister, mainly. My father died ten years ago. My mother's in Chicago now living with my aunt, and my sister's in Hawaii with her military husband and their daughter. I grew up here, moved away when I turned eighteen, then bought a condo uptown a couple of years ago when I decided I needed a home base to write from between trips."

"Sounds like an average background," she commented, toying with her salad.

He crumpled a napkin in his hand. "As a matter of fact, I come from a long line of miserable males and discontented females," he replied, avoiding her eyes. "Plenty of money, but little real joy. I learned early on that life is too short to spend it behind bars—emotional or otherwise."

He didn't know why he felt obliged to say that; it wasn't exactly a warning to her. Ryan had made it clear that she wasn't interested enough in him to require the usual carefully worded precautions about having lots of fun, but not making any promises.

"That wasn't the lesson I learned from my own life experiences," she said quietly.

"Oh?" he asked a bit too courteously. "And what valuable lessons did *you* learn?"

"That life doesn't mean much if you don't accomplish something worthwhile while you're here. It shouldn't all be fun and games."

"Didn't you enjoy your adventures overseas, Ryan?" he asked lightly.

She smiled. "I enjoyed it very much. My service with the Peace Corps has been the most-fulfilling experience of my life so far."

The Peace Corps. His smile faded. He'd assumed that her travel had been pleasure based, much as his own had been. Instead, she'd been out doing her part to save the world.

No wonder she had so quickly and naturally taken on responsibility for these two orphaned children she'd known only a matter of days. She was used to that sort of thing.

Keeping his expression only politely interested, he asked, "And are there any other lofty goals you've set for yourself—other contributions you'd like to make during this all-too-brief existence?"

"Yes," she replied simply. She didn't elucidate.

He figured she'd already demonstrated clearly enough that they couldn't be more different in their approach to life.

His attraction to her was still powerful, and he had a great deal of respect for her. But he knew better than to let it go any further than that. Max was the let's-have-fun-while-it-lasts type, Ryan was of the long-term-commitment persuasion.

Oil and water.

For now, they had a common goal: making sure no harm came to Pip and little Kelsey, and finding out what had happened to their missing aunts. Surely that was a noble-enough cause to satisfy even Ryan Clark for the moment.

When it was done, Max would move on, perhaps feeling a tiny bit of satisfaction that for once in his fairly hedonistic life he'd done something worthwhile.

6

RYAN WASN'T SURPRISED that Max lived in one of the more upscale apartment buildings in the city. He didn't ask her inside when she dropped him off; she wouldn't have accepted if he had.

"I'll call Juliana as soon as I'm inside," he promised. "Why don't you give me your home number in case I need to reach you?"

As she had with Mrs. Culpepper and Pip, Ryan wrote her number on the back of a business card. "You'll let me know as soon as she finds something?" she urged. "Or even if she doesn't?"

"I'll be in touch," he promised.

She nodded. "Max...thank you. It's reassuring to know I'm not the only one who cares what happens to Pip and Kelsey."

He smiled, oddly disconcerted by her words. "I'll call you," he repeated, and stepped away from the car. "Good night, Ryan."

"Good night, Max."

He didn't look back as he walked away from her.

MONDAY WAS LYNN'S day off from the shop, so Ryan and Cathy handled business that day. It wasn't as busy as it had been during the weekend, of course, but sales were still brisk. Ryan was glad to stay busy. It kept her from worrying all day about Pip and Kelsey—or worse, thinking about Max Monroe.

She took advantage of a midmorning lull to call her brother's office. He'd been out of town for the weekend, so she hadn't been able to reach him earlier. His secretary put her through. "Are you tied up for lunch tomorrow?" she asked as soon as he came on the line.

"I'm afraid so. Important luncheon meeting. But I'm free Wednesday."

She frowned, thinking of the deadline looming for the children. Thursday was the last day of the month, the day their rent was due. If the landlady hadn't heard from their aunt by then, she would call the authorities, and even Ryan had to admit she would be justified in doing so.

Worried by her silence, Nick asked, "What is it, Ryan? Is something wrong?"

"No, not really. It's just that I've run across a potential legal matter and I want to discuss it with you. But not over the phone."

"Listen, I can be at your shop in half an hour if—"

"Nick, it isn't an emergency," she assured him patiently. "I just want to talk to you, okay? Will you meet me for lunch at Juanita's on Wednesday? One o'clock?" Even if the children's aunt reappeared in the meantime, Ryan would still enjoy having lunch with her brother, she reasoned. It had been too long since she and Nick had gotten together.

"Make it twelve-thirty. I have to be in court by two."

"Fine. I promise I'll tell you all about it then."

"You'd better. You've got my curiosity aroused now."

Ryan smiled. "It's good for you. See you Wednesday, Nick."

Max called the shop an hour later. Ryan answered the phone. She was exasperated that her pulse rate automatically increased in response to his voice.

"I talked to my friend Juliana this morning," he said. "She's going to try to find some information for us about the children's aunts."

Ryan debated with herself for a moment, then shrugged

and decided to give her brother a thrill. She explained that she had set up a luncheon meeting with Nick on Wednesday, then asked Max to join them.

"Your friend, too, if she wants," she added. "I'd like to hear what she has to say, if she's found anything by then."

"Oh, she'll have something for us," Max assured her. "I'll set it up with her. I'll see you then."

"Yes," Ryan agreed, wishing she wasn't looking forward to it quite so much. How many times must she remind herself that she had no intention of acting on her unwelcome attraction to this man?

Climbed some of the highest peaks in the world…sailed in two international races…played polo with a prince and gone deep-sea diving with a famous news-magazine anchor. Jumped out of planes and off mountains, raced cars, bicycles and motorcycles…rodeo, downhill skiing and bungee jumping.

She could still hear Max casually listing all the adventures he'd had, could still remember the implied warning in his voice when he'd told her that he wasn't one to settle down or make long-term commitments. She'd known all along, of course—hadn't that been the reason she'd been so cautious with him? But to actually hear him say it…

She sighed. Max definitely did not fit into her plans. And she'd made them too long ago to change them now, no matter how tempting the short-term rewards might appear to her during moments of weakness.

She placed a call to Mrs. Culpepper after disconnecting with Max. A television blared loudly in the background when the landlady answered; Ryan recognized the theme music for a popular daytime serial.

She explained who she was, then asked if Mrs. Culpepper had heard from Opal yet. The landlady said that she had not. Ryan asked what time Pip and Kelsey usually got home from school.

"They get out at around two-thirty or so," the woman answered. "They walk home with some of their friends.

They stop at their friends' houses sometimes to play video games and do homework together. I tell 'em they have to be home no later than five."

Ryan figured she was going to have permanent teeth marks in her tongue if she talked to Mrs. Culpepper many more times. It was so difficult not to express her criticism of the woman's negligence in supervising the children. She kept quiet only because she was afraid the landlady would immediately call the authorities if Ryan annoyed her.

She hung up the phone with an ominous feeling that she had become involved in a situation that could get very unpleasant—and possibly painful—for everyone involved.

MAX STARED BLANKLY at the screen of his computer monitor. Amber letters marched like upright bugs across the black background; he had no idea at the moment what they spelled out.

He was having a hard time concentrating on Montana's adventures this afternoon. The reckless, dashing hero was probably quite disgusted with his creator, who'd spent the day dividing his thoughts between a dark-haired, dark-eyed doll-shop owner and two engaging, unfortunate orphans.

Montana, Max knew, would have put that troublesome trio behind him as fast as his nimble feet would have taken him.

Max, on the other hand, was fighting an almost irresistible urge to go to the mall. No matter how many times he'd promised himself he wouldn't get any more involved than he already was, he still found himself wondering if the kids had gone straight home after school or stopped by Ryan's shop. It was a cold day. Were they warm? Safe? Were they with Ryan?

Weird. He'd never given more than a passing thought to any kids he'd known before, including his own niece.

He could call Ryan and ask about them. Casually, of course. Or he could run over to the mall and check for himself. Surely there was something he needed to pick up while he was there. Underwear. Socks. Another baby doll for his niece.

He scowled. This was ridiculous. He was acting like a love-struck schoolboy—and love was one trap he had no intention of falling into. Just because his grandfather and father had thrown away all their dreams and led miserable, stiflingly boring lives didn't mean Max was genetically destined for the same fate.

He shuddered, thinking of how many times his grandfather had rambled on about all the trips he would have taken, all the sights he would have seen, all the adventures he might have had—if, of course, he hadn't married young and found himself with five kids to support.

Max's father had once dreamed of being a test pilot. He'd earned his pilot's license at the age of sixteen and regarded airplanes the way some people worship gold and diamonds. And then he'd met a pretty, blue-eyed blonde who'd teased, tempted and tied him into knots. The week after they'd graduated from high school, she'd announced with a mixture of embarrassment and satisfaction that she was pregnant.

Kevin Monroe had promptly abandoned his dreams of flight and had gone to work in his father's successful insurance firm, providing a good home for his wife and two children. He had then proceeded to work himself into an early grave. There hadn't been much time for flying, of course. And besides, it made his wife nervous when he risked his life—and her financial future—with that frivolous pursuit of cheap thrills.

Kevin had always assured Max that he didn't regret his marriage or his children. That he really liked his work in the insurance company. That he didn't mind sixteen-hour days or mind-numbingly boring meetings and society dinners. That golf was as adventurous a sport as any respectable, responsible married man could desire.

As for love—well, of course he loved his wife. Maybe it wasn't that heart-pumping, passion-fueled, soul-matched love of fiction and film, but it was...pleasant. Comfortable.

Max was quite proud that he'd managed to avoid the chains of love. No woman had ever tempted him to throw away *his* freedom, anchor *his* dreams to a four-bedroom house and a tax-deferred retirement plan.

Max lived on the edge—at least, most of the time. And if he'd found himself taking more and more of these stay-at-home intervals to work and enjoy the quiet pleasures of a morning newspaper and weekly football games in the park, well, that didn't mean he was getting old or settling down. He was just...resting.

Ryan's face came to his mind, so clearly that he could see the dimples at the corner of her shapely mouth, could almost picture the flecks of amber in her chocolate brown eyes. The clarity of the image made him decide to put her out of his thoughts and get back to work. He set his hands on the keyboard and scowled intently at the screen, trying to remember where he'd left off.

It was simply a case of attraction, he assured himself. She was a desirable woman, and he hadn't been involved with anyone for quite a while. It was only natural that he would be drawn to her. But that serious, commitment-embracing attitude of hers, that determination to follow her strict, long-term plans, combined with her involvement with the needy Coleman children—those were all sure signs that Max should keep his distance. A woman like Ryan could only be trouble for a man like him.

Montana would consider her more dangerous than the latest international terrorist he was pursuing through the deadly back alleys of a war-torn Middle Eastern city.

Max tended to agree.

RYAN WAS RATHER disappointed that Pip and Kelsey didn't stop by her shop on Monday afternoon. She spent a good part of the evening worrying about whether they'd gotten home safely. She thought of calling Mrs. Culpepper again, but was afraid of annoying the woman, who would only take her irritation out on the children. Surely the landlady would have called *her* if the children had failed to show up when they were expected.

She woke Tuesday morning thinking of Pip and Kelsey. And Max Monroe.

She told herself that she thought of Max only because he had somehow become connected with the children in her mind. She told herself it had nothing to do with the way he looked, or the way he smiled, or the seductive gleam in his warm, blue-gray eyes. The children were the only connection between herself and Max Monroe, she reminded herself firmly. Once they were safely settled, she would probably never see any of them again.

Her apartment seemed unusually quiet and empty as she ate her solitary breakfast and dressed for work.

It seemed lonely.

THE MORNING PASSED quickly enough. There was a great deal to do, with Christmas looming ever closer. To add to the excitement, Lynn came back to work with the jubilant announcement that she'd been to the doctor on her day off. She was pregnant.

Ryan squealed and hugged her friend, warmly congratulating her on the good news. She thought she did an admirable job of hiding her unbecoming ripple of envy.

She really was pleased for Lynn, who positively glowed with happiness. But Ryan couldn't help wondering if she would ever know that feeling herself.

It was almost three that afternoon when she looked up from her cash register just in time to see Pip and Kelsey enter her shop. She hurried to greet them with a smile.

"How was your day?" she asked them.

"Fine," Pip said with a shrug. "It's starting to rain,

though. We were afraid we were going to get wet before we got here. Do you mind if we stay for a little while until it stops?"

"I want to visit Annie," Kelsey said, already reaching for the dark-haired doll.

Ryan noticed in concern that Kelsey's cheeks and nose were red with cold, her hair damp from the drizzle falling outside. Her little jacket was pitifully inadequate against the cooler temperatures that were setting in as December approached.

"Don't you have a heavier coat, Kelsey?" she asked.

Carefully cradling the doll, the child shook her head. "Aunt Opal was going to buy me one, but she hasn't yet."

Ryan decided right then that she was buying the child a coat before the mall closed that evening. Pip, too. His was little better than Kelsey's. She knew she'd have to be careful not to hurt his pride, which was quite advanced for a child of his age. But somehow, she'd manage it.

"I'd better call Mrs. Culpepper," she said. "Let her know you're here so she won't worry."

Both children looked skeptical that their landlady would be concerned.

Ryan called anyway. As the children had expected, Mrs. Culpepper didn't react one way or another to the news that they were safe and dry. It was all Ryan could do not to slam the phone back in its cradle hard enough to leave the woman's ears ringing for a week.

Leaving Lynn in charge for a while, Ryan took her visitors down to the food court for a snack. They stopped by a children's clothing store on the way back up to her shop.

As she had predicted, Pip hesitated about letting her buy them coats. She soothed his concerns by implying that this arrangement had been made between herself and Mrs. Culpepper.

She felt guilty about misleading the boy, but then recalled the cold front that had been predicted to follow this evening's rain. She simply couldn't let Kelsey go off to school the next day in the thin, torn jacket that was all the child owned.

Kelsey was thrilled with the thickly lined, hooded purple coat Ryan helped her select. Pip chose a lined denim jacket, though he eschewed one with a hood.

Ryan was tempted to recklessly buy them entire wardrobes, as much as her credit card would provide. She restrained herself, keeping her purchases to a pair of warm gloves for each of them in addition to their coats, and a thick knit cap for Pip.

"Do either of you have homework?" she asked as they reentered her shop.

"I do," he admitted.

"Why don't you do your homework here? I'll call Mrs. Culpepper and tell her I'll drive you home later. Kelsey can help me around here until I can get away to take you home."

Ryan leaned over to whisper to Pip, "I really don't think Kelsey should be out in this wet weather. She could catch a cold or something."

Pip hesitated, then nodded. "Is there a table where I can put my books?" he asked, motioning toward the ragged denim backpack he'd dropped on the floor earlier.

"Of course. You can use the desk in my office."

"I didn't know you had an office," Kelsey said, looking around.

"It's in the back room. It has a computer and everything," Ryan said with a smile. "Would you like to come see it?"

The little girl nodded. "Do you really need me to help you today?"

"Of course. This is our busiest time of the year and Lynn and I have to wait on customers. We could really use help, um, straightening the dolls' dresses and hair," she improvised.

"I can do that," Kelsey said, looking delighted.

Ryan smiled. "I'm sure you can."

They really were sweet children, she thought as she led them toward her office. How could anyone not want the best for them?

AT JUST BEFORE 6:00 p.m., Ryan left her shop long enough to take Pip and Kelsey home. It was raining in earnest now; they huddled together beneath her umbrella as they ran up the sidewalk to their door. She took them straight to Mrs. Culpepper's, who had said on the telephone that their dinner would be ready when they got there.

Sending the children off to wash, Ryan turned to the dour-faced landlady, who smelled of the same beer and perfume she had before. "You haven't heard from either of their aunts?"

The woman shook her head. "Told you I hadn't when you asked on the phone," she reminded her. "Two more days and the rent is due. Had someone in today looking for an apartment, and I got no empties. I'm gonna have to rent it out unless next month's rent is paid—and I ain't renting it to a couple of kids I got to keep feeding," she warned.

Ryan nodded. "I understand. My friend and I are trying to locate their aunts. If you'll just be patient another day or two, I'm sure we'll come up with a solution."

"Yeah, well, I ain't been feelin' so good today. Think I'm comin' down with a cold. Gets any worse, I'm not gonna' feel like cooking for 'em. You'll either have to call someone or take 'em home with you until their aunts turn up."

Ryan swallowed. She'd already considered taking the children in, despite Max's grim warning of a potential kidnapping charge. She would ask Nick tomorrow what he thought of the possibility—at least until they found out what had happened to the aunts.

She had to admit the idea worried her. What did she know about taking care of two children, even on a temporary basis? Could she really do justice to both them and to her job during this hectic, busy season?

They hadn't been a bit of trouble today, but could they keep up their so-far-exemplary behavior? Wouldn't they quickly grow bored hanging around her shop, or following her rules when they were accustomed to taking care of themselves?

Freshly scrubbed, Pip and Kelsey reappeared. Ryan kissed Kelsey's cheek. The little girl clung to the embrace for a moment, then reluctantly stepped away. "Can I see you tomorrow?" she asked. "I can help at your shop again."

"Of course you may," Ryan assured her warmly.

"Now don't you be causin' any trouble for Miz Clark," the landlady warned indifferently.

"They aren't any trouble," Ryan said. "I have a television in my office they can watch if they get bored, and a big desk Pip can use to do his homework. I'll call you as soon as they get there, so you won't worry about them," she added a bit too politely.

"Oh. Yeah, do that. Er—thanks."

"Of course." Ryan turned to Pip. "Would it embarrass you too badly if I gave you a kiss, too?" she asked in a teasing whisper.

He grinned and presented his cheek. "Nah. Go ahead."

She planted a smacking kiss on his freckled skin and then ruffled his hair. "Good night, Pip. I'll see you tomorrow."

"'Bye. And if you see Max, tell him hi for me, okay?" The boy made the request with a casualness belied by the wistfulness in his eyes. A wistfulness that Ryan, unfortunately, could identify with.

"I will," she promised. "Good night, kids. Mrs. Culpepper."

She left quickly, needing to get back to work, but still fighting that reluctance to let Pip and Kelsey out of her sight.

"PIP? Are you still awake?"

The boy squirmed against his thin pillow. "Yeah."

From the other twin bed in their room, Kelsey cradled her motheaten old teddy bear against her little chest. She was just visible to Pip in the glow of the blue night-light plugged into a wall outlet. "When are we going to tell Ryan that we've picked her to be our new mommy?" she asked.

He winced. "I think we'd better wait awhile longer," he cautioned. "She's still getting to know us."

"Was I okay today? I tried to be as good as I could." Kelsey sounded worried.

"You were real good, Kelsey. I think Ryan likes you a lot."

"She likes you, too. I can tell."

Pip wasn't ready to be that optimistic. "Maybe." He sighed. "I wish we'd seen Max today."

"Max will be a good daddy. He'll teach you to play football, I bet."

"Yeah, well, first we've got to get him and Ryan together. She sure didn't say much about him today."

"No," Kelsey agreed thoughtfully. "But she smiled at him Sunday. I think she likes him. I bet they'd get married if we asked them to."

"That's not the way it works," Pip answered patiently. "He has to do the asking."

"He'll ask," Kelsey said with unwavering confidence. "Ryan's *beautiful*."

"Yeah. I think he likes her. We just have to be patient."

"I'll try," Kelsey murmured, starting to sound sleepy now. "But I wish they'd hurry. You said it's only four more weeks 'til Christmas and I want to spend it with our new parents."

Pip bit his lip, keeping his own wishes—along with his worries—to himself.

RYAN WALKED INTO Juanita's at twelve-twenty the next afternoon, scanning the crowded room for her brother or

Max. She didn't see either of them. She stepped to one side of the bustling reception area to wait for them.

Nick came through the door only minutes later. He greeted her with a smile and a kiss on the cheek. "Now what's this all about?" he asked, concern in his dark eyes.

She smiled and patted his arm. "Could we at least find a table first?"

He grimaced in apology at his characteristic impatience. "Sorry," he said. "You've got me curious."

"There will be two others joining us," Ryan told the hostess as they were led to a table. Max had called briefly that morning to confirm that he and Juliana West would be joining them. He'd implied that Juliana had some information for them; Ryan told herself that was the only reason she was so eager to see him.

"Two others?" Nick asked curiously, taking his seat.

"Yes. I have a surprise for you, Nick. Who's your favorite author?"

"Ian Fleming."

She rolled her eyes. "Make that your *second* favorite."

"M. L. Monroe."

She smiled in relief. "I was afraid we were going to have to go through a long list. Anyway, M. L. Monroe will be joining us in a few minutes for lunch."

"You're kidding."

"No. He answers to Max, by the way."

Nick leaned his elbows on the table, looking at her in surprise. "How did you meet him?"

"It's a long story—and part of the reason I wanted to talk to you today. But, basically, we met when he came into my shop to buy a doll for his niece."

"You mean the guy's local?"

"Yes. He has an apartment uptown. He's only here part of each year, when he's not off climbing mountains or jumping out of planes or playing tag with sharks or some other big adventure."

"I didn't even know he lived in this state," Nick said, shaking his head.

"He likes to keep a low profile, apparently. Says he doesn't care for publicity. I think he's afraid of being roped into social commitments," she added wryly.

She glanced across the room, then moistened her lips when her mouth went suddenly dry. "Here he is now."

Nick followed her gaze to the same hostess who had escorted them to their table and to the two people now following her. "Is that his wife?" he asked, a note of admiration in his voice. "She's certainly striking."

Ryan had already seen the woman at Max's side. As Nick had said, she was striking. There wasn't a man in the place who hadn't yet spotted her.

She was tiny—no more than five-two—but had a figure most women would have maimed for. Her hair was a rich, strawberry blond, falling almost to her waist in an untamed mass of tight curls. She was smiling up at Max in a way that made Ryan's fingers tighten spasmodically around her water glass. And he was smiling back at her.

"No," she said, her voice curiously flat. "She isn't his wife. She's a friend, he said."

"Mmm. I bet she is," Nick murmured appreciatively.

Ryan scowled.

Nick stood as Max and the woman reached their table. Ryan introduced Max and her brother.

"It's an honor to meet you," Nick said, looking sincere. "I enjoy your books."

Ryan noticed that Max looked a bit uncomfortable again at the mention of his books. He shook Nick's hand, thanked him quickly, then turned to his companion. "Ryan, Nick, this is my friend Juliana West. She's the private investigator I told you about, Ryan."

"Private investigator?" Nick asked, looking from Max to Juliana to his sister. "What is going on here, Ryan?"

Ryan motioned him back into his chair. "Sit down and we'll tell you."

Max seated Juliana next to Nick, then took the chair nearest Ryan. He smiled at her as he sat down; her bones seemed to melt in reaction. She straightened her spine with an effort, telling herself she really was getting ridiculous over this man.

She glanced at Juliana and found the woman watching them with bright, amused-looking green eyes. Juliana was younger than Ryan had expected. She couldn't be any older than Ryan, though she could have easily passed as a college student.

A waiter appeared with order pad in hand. They quickly made their selections.

The two men talked for a time about Max's books. Nick wanted to know if Max had actually lived any of Montana's reckless adventures, and the author admitted that he'd researched many of the daring sports he'd described through hands-on experience. Nick seemed fascinated by Max's brief recounting of some of those adventures.

Ryan found them a bit depressing, another pointed reminder that she and Max had little in common. She was quite sure that her suburban dream would hold little appeal for a man who risked his life regularly.

"Now," Nick said, when Max made it clear that he'd talked enough about himself and his career, "tell me what's going on. Why are we here today, Ryan?"

She drew a deep breath and started from the beginning, telling her brother about first seeing Pip and little Kelsey in her doll shop. She mentioned seeing them again at the mall food court the following day, and then having Kelsey show up unaccompanied when Pip had gone to the park.

She told her brother about the conditions the children were living under, about Mrs. Culpepper's indifference, about the uncertainty of the whereabouts of their guardian and the looming rent deadline. She confessed her concern for the children and her reluctance to contact the authorities on their behalf.

By the time Ryan finished, Nick was frowning heavily, his dark eyes grave. "You understand, don't you, that you're taking a risk getting personally involved with these children? Especially without notifying the proper authorities. Going to their apartment, putting them in your car, letting them hang around your shop—you could be opening yourself up for all sorts of trouble."

"Max has pointed that out several times," Ryan said dryly. "But surely you can't expect me to just turn my back and walk away when there's reason to believe these children need my help."

"No," Nick said in resignation. "I wouldn't expect that of you. So what do you want me to do?"

"I don't know yet," she admitted. "First maybe we should hear what Max and Juliana have to tell us."

They waited while their waiter set their lunches in front of them. And then Max picked up his fork and nodded to his friend. "Juliana, why don't you tell them what you've found."

Juliana referred to a small notebook, which she juggled efficiently as she spoke and still managed to eat. "Opal Coleman is thirty-nine, married once, took her maiden name back after the divorce, no children. Her brother and sister-in-law were killed in a plane crash near Dallas eighteen months ago, leaving her guardian of their children. There's one other sister, Essie Coleman Butternut Smith, age thirty-seven, divorced, no children.

"Smith's last known address was in Boston. I contacted her former employer there and learned that she'd been laid off due to company downsizing. No forwarding address as yet."

She consulted the notebook, full of what looked to Ryan like indecipherable chicken scratchings. "Opal Coleman quit an assembly-line manufacturing job here in town three weeks ago. Her co-workers said she hated the work, was always complaining about the long hours and low pay. They said she'd found a new boyfriend who talked big about moving to California and making a lot of money. They took off two weeks ago, supposedly to find a job and a place to live before sending for the kids."

"Did she ever talk about the children to her co-workers?" Ryan asked.

Juliana nodded. "Mostly complaining about what a big responsibility they were, and bemoaning the tragedy that made it necessary that she take them in. Her co-workers said she didn't seem to actively dislike the children, and no one believed she'd abused them, but she was definitely not a candidate for caretaker-of-the-year, if you know what I mean."

Ryan winced. "I'm afraid I do."

"And what the children told you about the plan to split them was true. The co-worker I talked to this morning said Opal had discussed that same course of action with her. She was planning on transferring guardianship of Pip to her sister and taking Kelsey with her to California. Apparently she knew the kids hated the idea and that they'd even threatened to run away rather than to allow it, but Opal seemed determined. I don't think her new boyfriend likes Pip. She said he thought the boy was too willful."

"Willful?" Ryan repeated indignantly. "If he meant that Pip is extremely mature and decisive for his age, well, yes, of course he is. He's had to be. He's been taking care of himself and his little sister for eighteen months."

Max touched Ryan's arm. "Listen to what else Juliana has to say."

She nodded, her arm tingling where he'd made contact. She ignored that disturbing sensation as she asked, "Have you found either of the aunts' current location?"

Juliana shook her head. "As I said, Essie moved without leaving a forwarding address—though we can probably assume that Opal knew where she was going. As for Opal herself…" She hesitated, then held up one hand in a gesture of bewilderment. "It's as if she disappeared off the face of the earth. She and her boyfriend were expected to meet with some of his friends in California. They never showed up. They aren't registered under their real names in any hotel or motel within a hundred-mile radius of the place where they said they'd be. She charged a tank of gas the day she left, but there have been no charges or bank transfers since."

Nick rubbed his jaw reflectively. "Sounds like maybe she and the boyfriend are in legal trouble. On the run from the law, maybe. I've seen similar cases a few times where people disappeared like this, usually because they had some reason for wanting not to be found."

"But the children…" Ryan said, frowning in confusion.

"We have to face it, Ryan," her brother replied gently. "From the evidence we've been given thus far, there's every reason to believe those kids have been abandoned— by both their aunts. If so, they will automatically become wards of the state."

7

"WARDS OF THE STATE." Ryan couldn't seem to stop saying it as she leaned against the wall of the service elevator heading up to the third floor of the mall.

She kept telling herself the words weren't as cold and intimidating as they sounded—but she couldn't make herself believe it. She was having a difficult time applying the term to the two children who'd so quickly stolen her affections.

"Ryan, your brother and Juliana promised to do everything they could to find out what's happened to Opal Coleman," Max reminded her. "We don't know for certain that the kids have been abandoned. And if they have, being wards of the state isn't automatically a bad thing. It only means that the courts become responsible for the children's welfare, seeing to it that they receive proper care."

"I know what it means," Ryan answered wearily. "I just don't like it. I'd rather take them home with me until we find out something conclusive."

"Your brother didn't think that was a good idea," Max responded. "Not without official permission of some sort. Maybe if Juliana can track down Essie Smith, she'll make a formal request as the children's aunt that you baby-sit them for a few days, or something along those lines."

Ryan nodded. "Maybe she will."

Max had followed Ryan back to the mall after lunch, when both Nick and Juliana had hurried away to keep previous appointments. He'd claimed he had some more shopping to do. Ryan didn't believe him, but hadn't bothered to argue. She hadn't been surprised when he followed her onto the elevator.

Santa Claus had stepped off just as Ryan and Max prepared to get on. The bearded man had greeted Ryan with a smile, a wink and the reassurance that the elevator seemed "well behaved" today.

She was thinking of him when the elevator bumped— just as it had the time she'd been stuck in it with him. She frowned and muttered, "Oh, no. Not now."

"What—?" Max began, but was cut off when the car jerked to a stop between the second and third floors. He reached out instinctively to steady Ryan when she stumbled. His hands lingered on her shoulders.

"It stopped," he said unnecessarily, staring at the frozen floor numbers.

"It did this the other day," she said with a sigh. "I was stuck in here for about ten minutes with, er, Santa Claus."

"How did you get out then?"

"I don't know. We pushed the alarm button a few times, then it just seemed to start up on its own. I've ridden it several times since without any problem. I assumed the proper repairs had been made."

"Did you report the incident to maintenance?"

Ryan cleared her throat. "No," she admitted. "I got busy and forgot. I guess I thought Santa took care of it."

Max shook his head and pressed the third-floor button, then the alarm button. Nothing happened either time.

He tugged at the collar of the white shirt he wore beneath a navy-and-green-plaid sweater. "How long did you say you were stuck in here last time?"

"Ten minutes, roughly." She eyed him warily. "Don't tell me *you're* claustrophobic."

"Not usually. It's just that I don't relish being stuck in an elevator."

"I know the feeling. I got pretty nervous when it happened to me last time."

"What did you do?"

"Santa distracted me," Ryan said with a wry smile, though she had no intention of repeating *that* conversation for Max.

"A distraction, hmm? Sounds like a good idea."

Something in his voice made her suspicious. She looked up at him just as he lowered his head and pressed his lips to hers.

If Max's goal had been to take her mind off the malfunctioning elevator, he succeeded amazingly well. In fact, his kiss cleared her mind of anything but him.

His lips moved leisurely, enticingly against hers, politely inviting her to join him.

Ryan might have resisted if he'd been more aggressive, more demanding. But she found it impossible to resist the hint of a smile in the curve of his lips against hers.

For just one weak moment, she closed her eyes and allowed herself to respond....

The kiss changed.

Sweetness turned to heat. Persuasion to hunger. Patience to greed.

Ryan found herself responding to each change with a growing fervor of her own. Her arms slid around his neck. His hands moved slowly from her waist upward, stroking, exploring, caressing.

She reminded herself that he was all wrong for her. That he didn't fit in to her plans.

But, oh, he felt so right.

Her heart fluttered. She jerked herself quickly out of his arms and moved away from him until she could feel the cool metal wall of the elevator through her green knit dress.

"I don't..."

She fell silent, unable to remember what she had intended to say.

"All in all," Max said, looking almost as dazed as she felt, "I would call that a fairly effective distraction."

Ryan gulped.

The elevator mysteriously chose that moment to move again.

Moments later, the doors slid open to reveal the third floor. An impatient-looking man waited there, one finger still pressed to the call button. He glared at Ryan and Max as they stepped out past him.

"Stopping the elevator to smooch," he muttered, dating himself with his phrasing. "How rude."

Her cheeks flaming, Ryan recognized the man as a sales-clerk from the sporting-goods store across from Beautiful Babies. He thought they had deliberately stopped the elevator between floors, she realized in embarrassment. Was it so obvious that Max had kissed her?

She resisted an impulse to lift a hand to her lips to check if they felt any different.

"Ryan," Max said, following as she turned and hurried toward her shop. "Wait."

"I have to get back to work now," she said without looking back at him.

"But I—"

She didn't pause long enough to let him finish.

Slanting a surreptitious glance over her shoulder, she saw that he stood outside for a long moment, frowning after her. Then he turned abruptly and walked away, his long, graceful strides carrying him swiftly out of sight.

"Was that Max you were talking to?" Lynn asked eagerly, craning her neck to watch him disappear into the crowd of shoppers.

Ryan forced a smile and nodded. "Yes. We were just talking about...about the children," she prevaricated. "Do me a favor, will you, Lynn? Call the mall office and report that the nearest service elevator seems to have a problem. Twice now it has stopped for about ten minutes between the second and third floors. Each time it mysteriously started again, but I'm afraid someone's going to be stuck in it for quite a while if repairs aren't made soon."

Lynn was fighting a smile. "You and Max were stuck in the elevator together?"

"Yes," she admitted coolly.

"You must have really hated that."

Ryan frowned. "This isn't funny, Lynn. There's obviously a malfunction with the elevator."

Lynn smoothed her expression, though her eyes were still suspiciously bright. "Who were you stuck with last time?"

Ryan sighed. "Santa Claus," she muttered.

Her assistant burst out laughing, abandoning her efforts to look sympathetic.

Ryan threw up her hands. "Just call the office, will you?" She stalked away, trying to look friendly as she approached a bewildered-looking customer.

"May I help you?" she asked, putting the recalcitrant elevator, her annoying assistant, Santa Claus and Max Monroe firmly out of her mind.

RYAN WAS BUSY with a customer when the children slipped in that afternoon. She didn't realize they were there until Lynn approached her, looking harried and wringing her hands. "It's little Kelsey," she said. "She's crying and we can't get her to stop. Something about a missing doll…?"

In sudden dread, Ryan glanced toward the shelf at the front of the store. She winced when she saw the noticeably empty space there.

She put a hand on Lynn's arm. "The dark-haired collector doll in the blue dress—do you know what happened to it?"

"I sold it late yesterday, after you'd left to take the children home," Lynn replied, looking concerned. "A nice older man bought it—for his granddaughter, I think he said. Why? Did I do something wrong?"

"No," Ryan said slowly, shaking her head and trying to look reassuring. She was kicking herself mentally; she'd honestly meant to set the doll aside for Kelsey as soon as she'd returned, but there'd been several customers before closing hour and she'd forgotten. It hadn't even crossed her mind again until now. "Take over here for a minute, will you, Lynn? I'll go see about Kelsey."

Lynn nodded, giving Ryan a look of sympathy.

She found Pip and Kelsey in one corner of the shop, the six-year-old weeping pitifully.

"C'mon, Kelsey, stop crying, okay? You knew somebody would buy the doll sometime," Pip was saying as Ryan approached. "There's lots of other dolls here to look at."

"But I want A-Annie," Kelsey sobbed. "She was my most fav'rite doll in the whole world."

"We'll find you another Annie," Pip promised rashly, looking desperate. "Surely there's another doll somewhere with dark hair."

"Not like Annie," the little girl mourned.

Ryan knelt by Kelsey's side. "Sweetie, I'm sorry. I didn't know the doll you liked had been sold."

Kelsey threw herself into her arms, sniffling. She seemed to be making an effort to stop crying. Distressed by the child's obvious heartbreak, Ryan held the little girl closely, smoothing her baby-fine hair.

"Sorry, Ryan," Pip murmured, his cheeks flushed. "We didn't mean to make trouble for you in your shop."

"You aren't a bit of trouble," she assured him.

She turned her attention back to Kelsey. "Why don't you pick out another doll? Any doll you want," she said heartily. "It will be my gift to you."

At the moment, she didn't care if Kelsey picked the most expensive, one-of-a-kind, artist-signed doll in the place. It would be worth the cost just to put the light back into those huge, despondent blue eyes.

Kelsey sniffed and wiped her nose on the back of her

hand. "Thank you, Ryan," she said politely. "But that's okay. I don't need a doll right now. Annie was s-special," she added in a broken whisper.

The knife twisted a bit deeper in Ryan's heart. She was ridiculously near tears herself.

"Then I'll do everything I can to find you another Annie," she said. "I'll call the manufacturer and order another one. An identical one. You won't be able to tell the difference. If they have another like her, of course," she had to add, unwilling to make a promise she might not be able to keep.

"Thank you," Kelsey said with a wan little smile. "But I don't think there is another Annie."

"Of course there is," Pip said, sounding a bit impatient now. "It's just a doll, Kelsey. Look around. There's zillions of 'em."

"Not like Annie," Kelsey repeated, her lower lip protruding stubbornly.

"Hey, what's going on? What's wrong?"

Ryan looked over Kelsey's head to find that Max had joined them.

Just what she needed, she thought with a mental sigh. Already her pulse had started pounding again at the sight of him. Her mind filled with heated memories. She gulped.

He looked at her questioningly, motioning toward Kelsey's tear-streaked cheeks. "Is there anything I can do?" he asked.

Pip's face lit up. "Max! Hi!"

"Hi, Pip," he answered, smiling and ruffling the boy's hair. "How's it going?"

"Pretty good," the boy replied. "Kelsey's crying 'cause someone bought her favorite doll."

Max glanced toward the empty shelf. "The one with the dark hair?"

Ryan wasn't sure how he'd known, but she nodded, still feeling guilty about the child's bitter disappointment.

"Lynn sold it while I was gone yesterday. I should have put it away."

Pip shook his head. "It's not your fault, Ryan. Kelsey knew the doll was for sale."

Kelsey nodded woefully and patted Ryan's cheek with a damp, chubby hand. "It's okay, Ryan. I'm not mad at you," she assured her.

That, of course, made Ryan feel even worse. She made a private vow to get on the phone immediately and try to find another doll.

"You two just get here from school?" Max asked.

Pip nodded. "We wanted to say hit to Ryan."

"I'm sure she likes seeing you," Max agreed. "Are you hungry? I was always hungry when I got home from school."

"I'm sort of hungry," Pip admitted.

Kelsey sniffed. "Me, too," she said. "A little."

"I'm hungry, too," Max assured them. "Why don't we go down to the food court and get something to eat? Then maybe we can go to the arcade and you two can teach me some new games."

"What about homework?" Ryan asked quickly. "Do you have any, Pip?"

The boy shook his head, obviously eager to go with Max. "I don't have any today," he said. "I did all my work at school."

"I don't have any, either," Kelsey seconded. "We don't get much homework in first grade."

"Let's go, then," Max said.

Ryan nodded. "I'll call Mrs. Culpepper and let her know you're here. You can leave your school things in my office. Your coats, too. You won't need them in the arcade."

"Those are nice coats," Max commented, looking from the children to Ryan. "Are they new?"

"Ryan bought them for us yesterday." Kelsey couldn't

seem to resist preening a bit in her new purple coat, her cheeks still damp from her tears.

"That was nice of her."

"We told her she didn't have to, but she wanted to," Pip said.

Max glanced at Ryan before speaking to the children again. "Go put your things away and we'll let Ryan get back to work."

Pip and Kelsey hurried toward the office. Ryan noticed with a pang that Kelsey looked wistfully over her shoulder at the bare shelf on which "Annie" had been displayed.

She groaned. "I can't believe I let that doll get away. I knew how much she loved it. I should have set it aside for her."

"Ryan, stop blaming yourself. You've already done a great deal for those kids. More than anyone could expect from you. You can't give her every doll in your shop, too."

"She didn't want every doll in the shop," Ryan murmured, thinking of Kelsey's polite rejection of her offer to choose any other doll she liked. "She just wanted that one."

Max touched her shoulder. "You're getting too involved," he said, looking worried now. "I'm afraid you're going to be hurt."

She looked at him and thought again of the shattering kiss they'd shared in the elevator. And she wondered if he knew it wasn't only the children with whom she was becoming too involved.

BUSINESS WAS RATHER brisk that evening, so Max took the children to their apartment, leaving Ryan to close up shop. Kelsey clung to Ryan's waist a bit longer than usual before leaving.

Holding the little girl tightly, Ryan felt the last of her objectivity slip away. She could no longer keep any emotional distance between herself and these children. In only a few short days, they'd firmly captured her heart.

Meeting Max's eyes over Kelsey's head, Ryan swallowed hard, knowing that there were dangerous cracks in her defenses where he was concerned, as well.

It was after ten when she got home. She was tired and emotionally battered, but too restless to attempt sleep. She wandered about her apartment, doing a bit of unnecessary housework, her thoughts torn between her concern for the children and her memories of a stolen moment in an elevator....

The doorbell chimed through the empty rooms, startling her into dropping the dust cloth she'd held.

She glanced instinctively at her watch. Ten-thirty. No one ever called on her this late without notice. She pressed a hand to her chest, imagining all sorts of grim possibilities. Bad news about her father or her brother. Something terrible happening to Pip and Kelsey while they'd been so vulnerably alone in their apartment.

She barely remembered to ask who was there instead of jerking open the door immediately.

"It's Max," he called softly in answer.

She opened the door slowly. "Max?"

Had something happened to the children? He looked so grave.

His eyebrows lifted in question when she didn't move or say anything. "May I come in?"

She stepped out of the way. "Is something wrong? Is there a problem with the children?" she couldn't help blurting out as she closed the door behind him.

He turned to face her, shaking his head. "I'm not here about the children, Ryan. This had nothing to do with them."

"Then why—?"

He moved a step closer to her, and she took a step back. "It's about what happened between us earlier. In the elevator. I can't stop thinking about it."

Her cheeks flamed. The huskiness in his voice took her back, made her remember the heat, the hunger, the ache....

"That—that was a mistake," she said, her own voice notably unsteady.

"Was it?" He was standing close enough to touch her now. He reached out to brush her warm cheek with the knuckles of his right hand. "It didn't feel like a mistake."

"Max, we hardly know each other." It was a weak point, but valid.

"What do you need to know about me before I can kiss you again?" he asked, his lips curving into a faint smile.

She frowned. "Don't laugh at me. I'm not trying to play games with you. I just don't want you to get the wrong idea about me. I'm not looking for an affair, or a fling, or a heavy flirtation, or anything else along those lines. I'm beyond that stage in my life."

"Ah, yes. Your Great Plan," he said, with just a hint of mockery underlying the words.

"I do have plans," she insisted, holding her chin up proudly. "I explained all this the other night. Life is too short to waste time—"

"Is having fun a waste of time, Ryan?" he interrupted gently. "Is it a waste of time to be with someone who makes you smile and gives you pleasure?"

She moistened her lips. "Well…"

He did make it sound awfully tempting.

He brushed his lips across her nose. He was standing very close, pressing lightly against her. His closeness wasn't threatening; she sensed that he would move back if she asked him to. Problem was, he felt so good against her that she didn't want to ask.

It had been a very long time since she'd felt this way, she mused. Her eyelids became heavy as she studied Max's handsome, smiling face. Maybe he and Lynn and Cathy were right. Maybe it wouldn't be so bad to have a little fun while she waited for her long-term plans to fall into place.

She placed her hands tentatively on his shoulders. "I

knew you were a heartbreaker the first time I saw you," she said rather sternly.

The corners of his eyes crinkled in that delectable manner. "Did you?"

She nodded. "I meant to keep my distance."

He moved an inch closer, just enough to make her shiver in response. "That would have been a shame," he murmured.

Little-boy mischief and grown-male temptation glinted in the depths of his gray-blue eyes. His lips curved into the devil's own smile.

She was going to regret this. She just knew she would. But tonight, she simply wasn't strong enough to resist him.

She rose on tiptoe and gave in to the almost overwhelming urge to brush her lips across that wicked smile. "Don't break my heart, Max," she whispered, the words escaping of their own volition.

"Don't let me," he advised her. Then his mouth settled firmly on hers, and whatever caution was left in her evaporated.

She wasn't changing her plans, she told herself. She was only making a slight detour along the way. A pleasure trip, of sorts.

Something she hadn't done in a very long time.

8

OH, MAX WAS GOOD. Much too good.

When Ryan gave an inch, he took a mile—so slickly, so smoothly that she didn't realize what he was doing until it was too late to protest. Until she'd gone too far with him to even want to protest.

She couldn't have said how they made it from her front door to her bedroom. Couldn't have explained what she'd been thinking to take him there.

Maybe she *wasn't* thinking. Only feeling.

And, oh, did it feel good.

She didn't know who removed the first item of clothing, who reached first for buttons and zippers and buckles. She only knew that Max's chest was broad and tanned and felt delectable against her breasts. That his skin tasted warm and slightly salty and utterly delicious against her lips.

She didn't know exactly which one of them made the first move toward the bed. By that time her mind was in a whirl and her body in such a state that it was a wonder she could remember his name. Or her own, for that matter.

Max didn't seem to be any more coherent.

He retained enough common sense to make sure there would be no unwanted consequences from their lovemaking. Later, Ryan would hope that she'd have thought of it if he hadn't.

Nothing had ever felt more right. More magical. She forgot her plans, forgot her worries, forgot that she'd known this man only a matter of days and that she'd never acted this way with anyone before him.

There was only one awkward moment. Max had just lifted his head from her breasts, leaving her moist and flushed and aching for total satisfaction. He crushed her mouth beneath his as he moved between her thighs. She shifted to welcome him, her arms wrapping around him hungrily.

Their eyes met as he surged inside her. And then they froze, their gazes locked. Ryan would have sworn she saw panic flare in his expression just as a wave of that same emotion crashed over her.

Maybe it all felt just a bit *too* right for comfort.

She bit her lip. He swallowed. And then he groaned and began to move again, whispering her name in a hoarse mixture of entreaty and warning.

Ryan let her mind go blank. She'd deliberately taken this path; now she was burning with impatience to see where it led.

It led to ecstasy.

IT WAS WELL after midnight when Ryan sat up in bed, the sheets drawn to her chin as she watched Max throw on his clothes. She was still dazed, and he seemed to be carefully avoiding her eyes.

Neither of them had said anything about what had passed between them.

Sliding his feet into his shoes, Max stood by the bed and ran a hand through his disheveled hair. "There's no need to get up," he said. "I'll see myself out."

She hadn't planned to get up. She wasn't at all sure her knees would have supported her if she'd tried. She nodded.

A bit stiffly, he leaned over and brushed a kiss across her swollen mouth. "I'll, er, call you, okay?"

She didn't wince, though she had to make an effort not to. His words just sounded so…hollow.

She nodded again. "Good night, Max," she managed to say, pleased that her voice seemed relatively normal.

"Good night, Ryan." He moved toward the open door. For a moment, she thought he would leave without looking back. And then he paused in the doorway, his face inscrutable as he turned. "Ryan?"

She swallowed. "Yes?"

"I didn't plan on you, either."

She sighed. "I know."

A moment later, he was gone.

Ryan buried her face in her hands as she heard her front door close behind him. She really should have stuck to the plan, she thought wearily. It would have been so much safer all around.

She didn't have time to waste on an affair that would lead nowhere. She didn't have time to nurse a broken heart after it ended.

So why did it now seem so inevitable that she would do both before the New Year dawned?

RYAN SPENT the morning avoiding her co-workers' questioning eyes and trying to pretend that her entire life hadn't changed in one reckless, impulsive, utterly magical evening.

She didn't hear from Max, nor did she expect to. She'd seen the wariness in him when he'd left her. It only helped a little to know that what had passed between them had been so powerful, so shattering, that it had affected him as well as her. It had obviously scared him into running for safety.

Pip and Kelsey stopped by the shop after school. Ryan welcomed them with a bright smile, her throat tightening when she noticed that Kelsey looked automatically toward the shelf where the little dark-haired doll had once been. Kelsey's answering smile wavered, but she didn't mention Annie.

Ryan was busy with some paperwork, but Cathy was ready for a coffee break. She volunteered to take the children down to the food court for snacks. "I'm kind of hungry myself," she told them.

Pip and Kelsey readily agreed. They seemed to like both Cathy and Lynn, though they obviously hadn't taken to either of them the way they had to Ryan and Max, for some reason. Ryan waved them off, telling them she'd call Mrs. Culpepper to inform her that the children had arrived safely.

Mrs. Culpepper answered the telephone on the fifth ring. Her voice was thick and surly. "I'm sick," she announced rather belligerently. "Told you a couple of days ago I thought I was gettin' a cold."

"I'm sorry. Is there anything I can do?" Ryan asked.

"Just keep them kids away from here. I don't feel like takin' care of 'em and they don't need to be around my germs, anyway."

Ryan bit her lip. "What do you want me to do with them?"

"I don't care," the woman answered wearily. "Take 'em home with you, I guess."

"But I don't have permission to do that."

"You got *my* permission. Opal left 'em with me, so I guess I'm in charge of 'em for now. You don't take 'em, I'm going to have to call the welfare services. Rent's due tomorrow, anyway, and I got people waitin' for that apartment."

"But, Mrs. Culpepper, I—"

"Look, you don't sound like you want to be bothered with 'em, and I can't say as I blame you. I should never have agreed to watch out for 'em, either. I'll call the welfare office now, tell 'em the kids got no place to go. They'll—"

"No!" Ryan said quickly, more sharply than she'd intended. "Don't call anyone. Please. I'll take them."

Mrs. Culpepper sniffed thickly. "You comin' after their stuff? I want that apartment cleaned out."

"The rent is paid through tomorrow, Mrs. Culpepper," Ryan reminded her coolly. "We have until then to pack their things."

"Yeah, well it better get done."

"You have my number if you hear from their aunt?" Ryan asked. "You'll call me?"

"Yeah, I got it. But I don't think I'll be hearing from her if I ain't heard by now."

Ryan privately suspected the woman was right. She didn't say so, however. She merely repeated that she wanted to be notified if anything happened, and then rather curtly concluded the call.

"Problem?" Lynn asked from nearby.

Ryan quickly summarized the call for her friend.

Lynn winced. "This is getting pretty sticky, isn't it? I hate to say it, Ryan, but it really does sound as though the children have been abandoned."

"I know," she whispered, making sure the few customers in the shop were out of hearing. "I don't know what I'm going to do."

Lynn looked worried. "The best thing to do would be to call the authorities."

Ryan scowled. "Everyone keeps saying that."

"Only because it's right."

Ryan shook her head. "I can't, Lynn. I can't just hand them over to strangers and forget all about them."

"Then what *are* you going to do?"

"For tonight, I'm taking them home with me," she said firmly. "I'm going to buy them both a few warm clothes and drive them to school in the morning. Maybe Nick or Juliana will have found something out before school is over tomorrow afternoon."

"Ryan." Lynn looked as though she were phrasing her words with care. "Are you sure you're being fair to the children? They're already so taken with you. What will happen when you have to let them go?"

Ryan hadn't thought of that. She opened her mouth to dismiss the question as irrelevant, but found that she couldn't brush Lynn's concern off quite so easily.

She moistened her lips, then lifted a hand in a bewildered gesture. "I don't know, Lynn. I guess I'll have to deal with that when we get there. For now, for some reason, they seem to need me. And I feel that I have to be here for them."

"I can see that you're very fond of them. That the three of you have bonded very rapidly. I'm just…well, I just want you to be careful. For the children's sake—and for your own."

Ryan nodded thoughtfully.

AS SOON AS CATHY returned with the children, Ryan ushered Pip and Kelsey into her office. "Mrs. Culpepper is ill," she announced, closing the door behind her. "She has a very bad cold and she's concerned that you two will catch it. She's asked me to let you stay at my place for a few days."

Kelsey's eyes grew comically wide. "We can come stay with you?" she asked in a little more than a whisper. "At your house?"

"At my apartment," Ryan corrected. "And, yes, you're welcome to stay with me. If you want to, of course," she added, turning again to Pip.

He looked anxious. "Are you sure we wouldn't be too much trouble? It's okay, you know. I can take care of Kelsey if Mrs. C. isn't feeling so good. I've done it before when Aunt Opal had dates and stuff."

The familiar ripple of anger surged through her; Ryan forced herself to ignore it. "I would love to have you," she assured him. "Really."

"But what about your work?" Kelsey asked.

"I'll take you to school in the morning and then come to the store," Ryan answered. "After school, I'll either pick you up or you can walk directly here."

She could always hire a sitter if the children grew bored,

she decided. She'd been staying after closing hours to stock the shelves and do paperwork, but she could work the stock during slow periods and take the paperwork home to complete after the children had gone to bed. Cathy had been hinting about coming to work for her full-time; Ryan could free up more hours for herself if she gave more responsibility to Lynn and Cathy.

It occurred to her that she was making a lot of plans, considering that she might not have the children for more than one night. She pushed the thought away, unwilling to dwell on the possibility.

"What do you say?" she asked, looking from Pip's cautious face to Kelsey's delighted one.

"Yes!" Kelsey said, then looked hesitantly at her brother. "It's okay, isn't it, Pip?"

"Sure," he said after a moment. "That sounds real nice."

Both Ryan and Kelsey heaved sighs of relief.

Ryan was rather amused that she'd found herself waiting as anxiously as Kelsey for Pip's approval.

"I have to get back to work," she said. "Why don't you watch television until dinnertime?"

She left them contentedly engrossed in a cartoon. She envied them their easy acceptance of their rapidly changing circumstances.

As for her—she was beginning to feel as though her life was spinning out of control, and that it would never be quite the same again.

LYNN PERSUADED RYAN to leave a little early that evening. "You have to stop and get the children's things, and Kelsey already looks sleepy," she insisted.

Ryan frowned. "I've been gone so much this past week. This is the worst possible time of the year for me to be away from work."

Lynn smiled and patted her arm. "Those children need you worse than I do tonight. I just talked to Jack, and he's on his way over to help me close up. And I called Cathy, as you suggested. She's delighted that you've asked her to come work full-time. She needs the extra money for Christmas. And her sister agreed to work part-time when we need her. It's going to work out just fine."

Ryan hoped her friend was right. She hoped the extra sales from Christmas shoppers would offset the extra expense of adding some twenty hours a week to Cathy's pay, as well as another part-time employee. But mostly, she hoped she'd done the right thing by getting involved with these two endearing orphans who'd wandered into her life only five days earlier.

Strangely enough, there was an almost inevitable feel to the whole situation. It was almost as though the children had been meant to find Ryan. As though she'd been waiting for them…

She didn't even want to think about how Max fit into destiny's plan.

Telling herself she must be more tired than she'd thought, she pushed her hair away from her face and smiled at Lynn. "I don't know how to thank you," she said simply. "But if there's any way I can do it, you're going to have a big bonus at the end of the year."

"I'm not doing anything for a bonus." Lynn wore a stubborn look. "This is my job, Ryan, and you are my friend. If you need me, I'm here for you."

Ryan's eyes burned, whether from emotion or weariness, she wasn't quite sure. She touched Lynn's hand. "Thank you," she said simply.

Lynn nodded. "Take the kids home and put them to bed. And then you might think of turning in yourself."

"I will. You get some rest, too. You're sleeping for two now."

Lynn chuckled politely at the lame joke and turned to help a customer. Ryan helped the children gather their things and ushered them out of the store.

She stopped by their apartment building on her way home to pick up some clothing for them to wear to school the next day. She looked around as they packed some things into paper grocery bags, the only luggage they had available.

There weren't many personal items in the place, she realized. It wouldn't take long to clean the apartment out for the tenant Mrs. Culpepper supposedly had waiting.

What should be done with Opal's things? Who would be responsible for them if no one showed up to claim them? What would happen to the children?

Trying to push her worries out of her mind, Ryan forced a smile for the children, who'd emerged from their bedroom with their little arms loaded. "You have everything you need? pj's? Toothbrushes? Clean underwear?"

"We have everything," Pip said confidently.

"I'm sure you do," Ryan said, conceding to his competence.

Though not as upscale as Max's place, the apartment complex where Ryan lived was in a nice neighborhood made up mostly of young working singles and newlyweds. Pip and Kelsey looked wide-eyed at the impeccable landscaping, the closed-for-the-season pool, the tennis courts and the picnic tables set out for outdoor entertaining when the weather was warm. Cheery Christmas decorations were strung everywhere, and many of the apartment windows were already filled with glowing Christmas trees.

Moderate though the complex was, it was still a far cry from the dingy, run-down building where Pip and Kelsey had spent the past eighteen months.

"Do you have a Christmas tree, Ryan?" Kelsey asked, pointing to a brightly colored one in an apartment near Ryan's parking space.

"Not yet. I haven't had time to get one yet. I had hoped to be able to put one up this weekend."

"Maybe we can help you," Kelsey suggested, her sleepy eyes glowing. "We didn't have one last year. Aunt Opal said it wasn't worth the trouble."

"Of course you can help me," Ryan declared recklessly, ignoring a twinge of misgiving. She promised herself that whatever happened during the next few days, she would find a way to have Pip and Kelsey help her with her tree.

She'd put her tree up alone last year. And then she'd found herself wiping tears from her cheeks, keenly aware that Christmas wasn't a time to be by yourself. Christmas was a time for family. For children.

Maybe this year she wouldn't be alone.

Still struggling with her doubts, she unlocked the front door of her ground-level apartment. "Here we are," she said. "Make yourselves at home."

The children almost tiptoed into the apartment, looking around with shy curiosity. Ryan tried to see the place through their eyes. The Shaker oak furniture. The country decor—Amish prints, hand-crocheted afghans, colorful pillows, antique oil lamps on the mantel. A few hand-crafted items she had picked up on her travels.

Far from elegant, of course—Ryan couldn't afford elegance. But it looked like a home.

"It's beautiful," Kelsey whispered.

Ryan smiled. "Thank you."

She led them into the spare bedroom, which was furnished with the twin-bed set that had been in Ryan's room when she was growing up. Her father had given it to her—along with her oak dining set and a few other pieces—after her mother died, when he'd moved into an apartment building for senior citizens.

"My room is just across the hallway," she said. "I'll be able to hear you if you need me in the night."

She knew they were accustomed to spending nights alone, with no one but each other to depend on, but she wanted them to know it wasn't that way tonight. Someone cared about them now. Cared very deeply about them. So much, in fact, that it scared her.

"We'll be fine," Pip assured her.

"I know you will, Pip," Ryan told him with a rueful smile. "But I'll still be here."

The children brushed their teeth, changed into pitifully ragged nightwear and crawled into the beds. Ryan tucked Kelsey in, making sure her old teddy bear was nearby. And then she leaned over to kiss the child's freshly washed cheek. "Good night, sweetheart. Sleep well."

Kelsey was smiling. "This is nice," she murmured, already half-asleep. "You make a very good mommy, Ryan."

Ryan felt her heart jerk. "I—er—good night, Kelsey."

"'Night." The child snuggled into the soft pillow, her teddy bear in her arms, and closed her eyes.

Still shaken, Ryan turned to Pip, who was watching her solemnly from his own bed. She wondered if he considered himself too old and self-sufficient to be tucked in. She moved close to his bed, looking down at him. "Do you need anything else?"

He shook his head. "I'm fine. Thank you."

Ryan wanted very much to take him in her arms and tell him it was okay to be a little boy again. That he wasn't alone now. She contented herself with a quick kiss on his cheek. "Good night, Pip."

"'Night, Ryan. Thank you again. For everything."

Her smile felt tremulous. "You're welcome."

She left the bedroom door open a few inches, just so she could hear them if they needed her during the night.

She had to acknowledge, if only to herself, that it felt good to be needed.

IT WAS JUST AFTER TEN when the telephone rang. Ryan had been sitting on the edge of the bed, smoothing moisturizer on her legs, preparing to turn in. She snatched up the phone before it could ring a second time and disturb the children. "Hello?"

"Hi. It's Max."

The plastic bottle of moisturizer fell unnoticed to the carpet. "Oh. Hi."

"I, uh, just called to see how you are."

"I'm fine. And you?" If he could be bewilderingly polite, so could she.

"Yeah. Fine. Um, did you hear from the kids today?"

"They're with me now. They're asleep." She told him what had happened.

"What are you planning to do with them tomorrow?" Max asked after he'd gotten over his initial surprise that she'd taken the children in.

"I don't know," Ryan admitted. "It's the last day their rent is paid, and Mrs. Culpepper insists she wants everything out of the apartment by tomorrow evening. If we haven't heard from one of the aunts—well, I just don't know what I'm going to do."

"You haven't reconsidered calling the child welfare services?"

"No. I can't call them. Not yet."

"So what are you going to do?"

"I'm going to keep them with me. At least until we find one of their aunts."

Max paused a moment. "Okay," he said finally. "I'll tell Juliana that speed is of the essence. Not that I'll have to—she's pretty compulsive when it comes to a challenging case."

"You've, um, known her awhile?"

"Since she was a toddler. Her older brother was my best friend."

"Was?"

"He died." Something in the stark words told Ryan not to ask any further questions.

"I'm sorry."

"Yeah. Me, too. I guess I'd better let you go. I'm sure you're tired."

"Yes. I was just about to go to bed."

The pause stretched longer this time. Ryan moistened her lips.

When Max spoke again, his voice sounded just a bit husky. "Sleep well."

"Good night, Max."

Her hand wasn't quite steady when she hung up the phone. She climbed beneath the covers, turned off the lamp and lay in the darkness, achingly aware of how empty her bed seemed tonight—and wondering if Max would ever kiss her again.

9

RYAN RECEIVED A RESPITE of sorts the next day. Though she dreaded doing it, she called Mrs. Culpepper midmorning to talk about the apartment. The landlady told her that she'd already rented the place, then added that the new tenants had put down a deposit, but wouldn't be moving in until the middle of December.

"You've got that long to clean it out," she added. "After that, I'm going to have to get rid of the stuff."

"You're being very generous," Ryan said, though it galled her to say so. "We're doing everything we can to locate Opal and Essie, and I promise we'll let you know as soon as we hear anything."

"Yeah, okay. You're takin' care of the kids?"

"Yes, I'm taking care of them," Ryan said, softening a bit. At least the woman had asked about the children, whether she was sincere or not. "How are you? Is your cold any better?"

"Not much," she replied, sniffling. "But I'll be all right. Got somethin' here to take for it."

Ryan was sure she did. Probably the kind of "medicine" that came in a bottle wrapped in a brown paper bag. And then she chided herself for being ungracious. "I'll be in touch," she promised.

The next number she dialed was her brother's office. "I have the children," she told him, and then explained the situation.

Nick sounded resigned. "I didn't think it would be long

before you took them home with you," he admitted. "So I've been calling in some favors. I have legal permission for you to take care of the kids for the next couple of weeks, or until one of the aunts is located."

"You do?" Ryan asked, startled. "But how—"

"The juvenile judge is a good friend of mine. As I said, he owes me a few. This isn't permanent, you understand, and you have no real authority when it comes to the kids. You're simply the official baby-sitter for a couple of weeks."

"Nick, thank you. I've been so worried about them."

"I know you didn't want the authorities notified, but I couldn't let you get slapped with a kidnapping charge. But, Ryan, if their aunts haven't shown up in a week or two, you're going to have to turn them over to the social workers. You understand that, don't you?"

"I'm sure Juliana will find something before then," Ryan insisted, trying not to think that far ahead. "In the meantime, at least I'll know the children have a safe place to stay."

"What about your job? This has to be a busy time of year for a doll shop."

Ryan told him about hiring Cathy full-time, and about Lynn's generous offer to help.

"And I'll probably hire someone to watch the kids in the evenings," she added. "I can't keep them here at the shop every night. Not only would they be bored to tears, but Kelsey needs to be in bed earlier than that. I'm thinking about asking my neighbor. She's a newlywed and her husband works nights, so she's at loose ends right now. She loves children, and I'm sure she wouldn't mind the extra money."

"I'll pay her."

"That isn't necessary. You haven't even met the children."

"I know. But I want to help. Call it my good deed this Christmas, okay?"

"Nick—"

"Ryan," he interrupted, "it's settled. You talk to your neighbor. I'll pay her."

She sighed, then smiled. Her older brother had always been a softie beneath his sometimes-impatient exterior. "Thanks, Nick."

"Yeah, well, I keep thinking that Pip and Kelsey are about the same difference in age as we were. We were lucky to have two parents who loved us and were around to take care of us when we were little."

Ryan knew that if anything had ever happened to their parents, Nick would have watched out for her as carefully as Pip was taking care of Kelsey. Maybe Nick had thought of that, as well. "You'll have to come by and meet them," she told him. "They're really cute kids."

"I'll do that. Er—have you heard anything from Juliana?"

"No. Max was supposed to call her and let me know if she'd found anything."

"Maybe I'll give her a ring myself. Just to check on her progress, of course."

Ryan smiled and cocked her head. "Do I hear a note of personal interest in your voice?"

"She *is* attractive," Nick admitted, a smile in his voice. "You're sure she and Max aren't—"

"They're friends. A brother-and-sister relationship, apparently."

"Yeah, that's the impression I got. In fact, it seemed to me that Max was most definitely interested in you."

"The only thing between Max and me is that we both accidentally became involved with Pip and Kelsey," Ryan lied. "Once they're settled, he'll be off on another of his exciting adventures."

That part, she thought grimly, was true.

"Hmm…"

"Call Juliana, Nick," Ryan said abruptly. "You'd make a cute couple. Now I have to get back to work."

RYAN DIDN'T HAVE a chance to eat lunch that day. Business was steady, and even with Cathy there to help out it got hectic at times. She made sure both Lynn and Cathy took lunch breaks, but she used her own time catching up on the paperwork she would usually have done after business hours.

She took a quick break with the children when they arrived after school. They went down to the food court for cookies and juice.

The Christmas-village display was nearby as well as the usual long lines of children waiting for to ride on the train and to talk to Santa. Kelsey waved to the bearded man as she sat down at the table Ryan had selected. "I like his eyes," she said. "They twinkle."

Pip grinned conspiratorially at Ryan. "They're supposed to twinkle, aren't they, Ryan?"

"Of course," she agreed. "He wouldn't be Santa Claus without twinkly eyes."

"I sure hope he gets me what I want for Christmas," Kelsey murmured, gazing at him wistfully.

Wondering if Kelsey had asked for the doll she'd named Annie, Ryan bit her lip. She had been trying all day to locate another one like it. So far she'd had no luck at all.

THE CHILDREN WATCHED television in the office and then played with a board game Ryan bought them on the way back to the shop. She checked on them whenever she had a minute, but they seemed to be getting along just fine.

She'd noted that they rarely quarreled, which seemed unusual for siblings their ages. And then she thought that perhaps they got along so well because it had been so long since they'd had anyone but each other to turn to. The thought made her sad.

At just after six, Lynn and Cathy cornered Ryan.

"Take the children and go home," Lynn said, her tone

brooking no argument. "Spend the evening with them. They need you."

She hesitated. "It's going to be busy tonight. Are you sure you can manage everything without me?"

"Hard as this may be for you to believe, we'll get along just fine," Lynn assured her with a smile. "Those kids need your attention this evening."

"I don't know what I would do without you," Ryan said, touched by their consideration.

"Neither do we," Lynn quipped. "Now go."

KELSEY AND PIP SEEMED pleased with the idea of spending the evening with Ryan. She stopped at a supermarket on the way home to buy supplies for dinner and asked them if they wanted anything special for either dinner or breakfast. They seemed surprised to be consulted. Both assured her that anything would be fine.

Again Ryan was struck by their reticence in asking for anything. Other children in the market were begging their mothers for particularly well-advertised brands of cereal or candy from the temptingly located displays at the checkout lanes. Pip and Kelsey, she mused, were so accustomed to not having special treats that they never even considered asking.

Dinner was almost ready when Ryan's doorbell rang. The children were washing up, so Ryan wiped her hands on a dish towel and went to answer the door. She had to clear her throat before she spoke, suspecting the identity of the person on the other side. "Who is it?"

She was right. "It's Max."

Her mouth went dry. She had to draw a deep breath before opening the door.

Max stood in the hallway, his arms loaded with packages. His expression was almost grim. "Your friend at the store told me you were spending the evening at home. Where are the kids?"

"Washing up for dinner. Why?"

He looked around quickly, as though checking to make sure the children weren't within hearing range. "Juliana called. There's a chance Opal Coleman has been found."

"Found? Where?"

"Southern Utah. But it isn't confirmed yet."

Something in the set of his jaw made her stomach clench. "What do you mean by confirmed?"

His eyes met hers squarely. "We're waiting on dental records."

Ryan closed her eyes. This was one possibility she hadn't considered.

How would they tell the children?

"Max! Have you come to have dinner with us?" Kelsey squealed from behind them.

Ryan whirled. She was relieved to see that Kelsey's expression held nothing but surprised pleasure. Obviously, the child hadn't overheard anything to concern her.

Max smiled. "Hi, Kelsey. I brought you and Pip some things."

Ryan suddenly realized that she'd kept him standing in the doorway. She flushed and motioned for him to come in.

As he passed her, he murmured, "I'll tell you everything later, okay?"

She nodded and managed a weak smile. "We were just about to eat. You'll join us, won't you?"

"I'd like that," he said. "If you have enough, of course."

"I made plenty," she assured him.

He nodded and their gazes locked. Ryan saw the memories reflected in his eyes—memories of the last time he'd been here. She shivered as similar thoughts filled her mind.

Kelsey was eyeing the packages in Max's hands. She shifted from one foot to the other, obviously wanting to ask about them, but trying to be polite about it.

Pip joined them then. He seemed even more delighted to see Max than his sister had been. Ryan realized that Pip must be hungry for male attention, especially if his aunt's boyfriend had been distant and disapproving.

What would happen to these children if their aunt was really dead? Would their other aunt, if she could be found, be willing to take them in? Could she provide a good home for them and the security they so obviously longed for?

"I have some things for you both," Max told the children, dumping the stack of packages on the couch. "A friend of mine works in a children's store and she has a sales quota to meet, so I thought I'd help her out."

Her, Ryan thought wryly. Just how many "friends" did Max have, anyway?

Not that it was any of her business, of course, she reminded herself hastily. No matter what had passed between them, she and Max certainly weren't a couple. They'd made no commitments to each other, nor did she expect any.

Pip and Kelsey moved closer to Max. Ryan stationed herself nearby, almost as curious as the children about what the packages held.

With the flourish of a magician producing small furry animals from a hat, Max began to open the packages. He pulled out clothing—sturdy jeans, colorful sweaters, trendy screen-printed sweatshirts. Warm pajamas. Socks and underwear. A red dress with a white lace collar for Kelsey.

"We had to guess the sizes," he said. Glancing at the children's grubby sneakers, he added, "My friend said there was no way to guess about shoe sizes, though. You'll have to try them on. We'll go tomorrow and find you some new shoes."

"But, Max," Pip said, looking rather longingly at the clothing. "This stuff is really expensive."

Kelsey touched the red dress with a look of awe. "They're beautiful," she whispered. "I've never had so many new clothes all at one time."

"Let me do this, Pip," Max said, meeting the boy's eyes with a man-to-man air. "I really want to."

Pip bit his lip. "Aunt Opal said we don't take charity."

"It isn't charity. It's a gift. From a friend."

Pip hesitated another moment, then glanced at Kelsey, who was watching him anxiously. He made a rueful face and shrugged. It was an oddly grown-up gesture. "Thank you," he said gravely.

"You're welcome," Max replied, just as seriously.

For some reason, Ryan felt a lump form in her throat.

Max had one more bag. From it, he pulled a handheld video game with several game cartridges for Pip, and an electronic first-computer game for Kelsey. "It talks," he explained to her. "It has a lot of games loaded into it."

Kelsey stared at the toy with huge eyes. "Thank you," she said. "It's really cool."

Max smiled. "We'll figure out how to work it after dinner, okay?"

"Why don't you take your things to your room now while I get the food on the table," Ryan suggested. "Dinner will be ready in just a few minutes."

"I'll help you," Max offered.

She nodded. "Thank you."

Alone in the kitchen, she turned to him. "You were very generous."

"I wanted to help out," he said with a shrug. "It's easy enough to buy things for them. You're the one who's taken them in, sacrificing your valuable time for them."

"I don't consider it a sacrifice," she said. "Tell me what Juliana found out."

He exhaled. "A car was found at the bottom of a ravine on a long stretch of highway in southern Utah. Authorities estimate that it had been there for at least a week before it was discovered. It must have gone off the road at night, when no one was around. It exploded and burned."

Ryan's fingers tightened compulsively around the dish she'd picked up. "And no one saw it for a week?"

"Apparently not. At least, no one who bothered to report it. As I said, the area was very isolated, and there was heavy brush at the bottom of the ravine. In addition to that, there have been heavy rains there during the past week."

Ryan drew a deep breath. "Opal Coleman was in the car?"

"She and her boyfriend, apparently. As I said, they're waiting on dental records to be sure. The Utah authorities have been trying to identify the bodies for several days."

Ryan set the bowl down and leaned heavily against the counter. "What happens now?"

"We intensify the search for Essie Smith. Juliana has a couple of leads. She'll pursue them tomorrow."

"Should we tell the children?"

He winced and shook his head. "I wouldn't," he said. "Not until we know something for sure. They're already uncertain enough about their future. This could only worry them more."

"I think you're right." Ryan explained Nick's arrangement for her to keep the children until relatives had been found. "I talked to my neighbor this afternoon. She's willing to watch them in the evenings until I get home from work. At least we'll know they're being well cared for until permanent arrangements can be made."

"From everything Juliana's found out about Essie Smith so far, she isn't a very stable person." Max sounded grim again. "And now she's out of a job, as far as we know. The future doesn't look very promising for the kids, I'm afraid."

Ryan pushed a strand of hair away from her face. "Maybe she'll give them up for adoption," she mused aloud.

Max's eyes widened. "Surely you aren't thinking of—"

"No, of course not. I didn't mean *me*," she said, startled that he'd jumped to that conclusion. "I meant to a good home, where they'd have two parents and a stable environment."

"Oh." He nodded. "That would certainly be best for them. I've heard, though, that most adoptive couples want younger children."

"Anyone who'd take the time to meet Pip and Kelsey would have to realize how adorable they are," Ryan said wistfully. "Surely anyone who wants children would love to have those two."

The conversation was interrupted at that point when the children rejoined them. Ryan hastily set the table with an extra plate for Max, and they sat down to eat.

Max seemed determined to keep them all entertained during dinner. Kelsey giggled frequently, and even Pip laughed aloud a time or two.

No one seemed to notice that Ryan was a bit quiet.

She couldn't stop thinking about Max's assumption that she'd been talking about adopting the children herself. It was a crazy idea. Too implausible to even consider.

Wasn't it?

AFTER DINNER, Ryan popped corn and the four of them settled in the living room to watch Christmas specials on television.

Max seemed in no hurry to leave. Ryan couldn't help wondering if he was bored. Watching "Frosty the Snowman" and "Rudolph the Red-nosed Reindeer" hardly compared to climbing mountains and swimming with sharks.

But if he was bored, he certainly didn't show it. In fact, he startled her and delighted the children by quoting several lines from both the specials, which he claimed to have seen every Christmas since he was just a kid himself.

Afterward, Max stayed to help Ryan tuck the children into bed. He kissed Kelsey and ruffled Pip's hair, assuring them both he would see them again soon.

Ryan kissed and hugged Kelsey, then brushed her lips across Pip's cheek.

"Good night," she told them both from the doorway. "Sleep well."

"'Night, Ryan," Pip said.

"This has been nice," Kelsey said, as she had the night before. Only this time she added, "Like a real fam'ly."

Ryan tried to ignore the sudden hollow feeling in the pit of her stomach as she ushered Max out of the room.

"Would you like some coffee before you leave?" she asked. Her voice sounded a bit too loud in the silence now that the children were in bed.

"Before I leave?" he repeated. "Does that mean you're ready for me to go?"

"You're welcome to stay awhile longer, of course. But— well, the children are here," she explained needlessly.

He frowned. "I'm aware of that. I didn't expect…" He let the sentence trail off.

She smoothed her slacks with her hands. "So *do* you want coffee?"

He hesitated, then shook his head. "I'd better go. You have to be up early to get the kids ready for school. I'll call you tomorrow, after I talk to Juliana."

"All right." She walked him to the door. "Good night, Max."

He put out his hand and tipped her chin upward, so that she was gazing up at him. He seemed to be studying her eyes, looking for—what? Whatever it was, she couldn't tell whether he found it.

He brushed his mouth lightly across hers. He didn't linger long enough for her to respond. "When the children are settled somewhere, we need to talk," he murmured.

She almost asked what he wanted to talk about, but she changed her mind at the last minute.

"Good night, Max," she said again, a bit huskily.

"Good night, Ryan." He left without further delay.

She closed the door behind him, then stood for a long, motionless moment with her forehead pressed against the cool wood.

MAX PACED THE LENGTH of his apartment again. He didn't even pretend to work this time.

He could still feel her mouth beneath his, though he'd kissed her only lightly this evening. He hadn't trusted himself to do more.

What was it about Ryan Clark, he wondered, that he couldn't stop thinking about her? He tried to figure it out. Tried to dissect his interest in her with cool detachment.

Her large, dark eyes. Her smooth, oval face. Her kissable mouth. Her lush dark hair. Her slim, supple body...

He cleared his throat, shoved his hands in his jeans pockets and moved on to the next point.

He'd only known her a week. Then again, he'd become involved with other women on such brief acquaintance. Instant attraction. Carefree passion. A short time of mutual pleasure with no strings, no regrets afterward. Granted, it had been years since he'd indulged in such behavior. But it *had* happened.

Not that he'd ever had any of the feelings he'd experienced when he'd made love with Ryan.

The lovemaking had started out the same way it had in the past. He'd desired her, had sensed an answering attraction in her and had naturally followed up on those feelings.

But sometime between that first practiced kiss and the unprecedented explosion that had followed, something had changed. Something that had scared the life out of him.

He hadn't worried that those other women could change him or threaten all the decisions he'd long ago made for himself.

Ryan worried him. No. Ryan *terrified* him.

He told himself he should stay away from her. Of course, for now, they were both involved with the kids.

Max realized he had no real obligation to them—his connection was tentative at best. But, like Ryan, he'd been unable to walk away.

Maybe it was the way Pip looked at him, as if the boy saw something in Max that few others could see. Maybe it was Kelsey's sweet, trusting smile.

Or maybe it had something to do with Ryan....

No, he wouldn't leave yet. Not until something had been decided about the kids.

After that—well, he didn't know. Would it be possible for him to spend time with Ryan Clark without giving too much of himself? Could he make love to her again without losing himself in her?

Oh, yeah, Ryan was different from those other women—the ones who'd enjoyed their time together, no matter how brief, and then walked away without a backward look.

Even more worrisome, Max was beginning to wonder if *he'd* be able to walk away quite so easily this time.

MAX CALLED RYAN at her shop early Saturday morning. "It's been confirmed," he said without preamble. "Opal is dead."

Ryan sagged against the counter. "Oh, Max."

She wondered how the children would take this new tragedy in their young lives. They had spoken very little of their aunt, and Ryan had gotten the impression that their relationship with her hadn't been particularly close. But how would her death affect them?

"Ryan?" Max said, reminding her that he was still on the line.

"I'm here."

"What now?" he asked. "What are you going to do?"

"I'll call Nick and tell him what you've learned."

"Juliana was going to call him. I'm sure he already knows."

"Oh. Well, I'll call and see what he recommends that I do now."

"What do you *want* to do?"

Ryan bit her lip. "I want to keep the children a little longer," she said. "At least until their other aunt is found. I don't want them going to strangers."

To his credit, Max didn't point out that she was little more than a stranger to them herself, though she knew he would be justified in doing so. She was all the children had now; somehow, she would find a way to be there for them.

"Ryan…" Max sounded worried.

"I know what you're going to say—that I'm getting too involved with them. But I can't help it, Max. They need me."

His sigh was just audible through the phone lines. "Yeah. I sort of thought you'd say that."

"I can't help it."

"I know." He brought the call to a rather abrupt end. "I'll talk to you later."

Ryan found it easier not to think of the future, at least as far as Max and the children were concerned. She concentrated instead on how much pleasure she found in having Pip and Kelsey with her now.

They were so well behaved. So bright and funny.

How could anyone not love them?

It was an extremely hectic Saturday at her store, as Christmas shoppers turned out in droves. The neighbor who'd agreed to baby-sit weekday afternoons had other plans, so Ryan had been forced to take the children to work with her. They played quietly in her office most of the day, content to take a quick lunch break with her and then entertain themselves again.

Max showed up midafternoon and took the children off for a few hours of fun in the mall—a movie and an hour of arcade games. Ryan was touched that he'd bothered, a bit confused by his motives, and secretly envious of the leisure time he was able to enjoy with them. Just when *did* he work, anyway?

Sunday was usually Ryan's day off. She would have liked to take the children to church with her, but she wasn't ready to face the inevitable questions from her friends. How would she explain her current relationship to them?

With business so heavy, she didn't feel comfortable taking the entire day off, so she compromised by leaving the children with her neighbor while she worked for four hours that afternoon. Pip made it clear that he saw absolutely no need for her to hire a baby-sitter each time she left them; he even seemed a bit insulted that she did so.

It was the first time he'd questioned Ryan's authority.

Ryan tried to soothe his injured pride, but she stood firm on her decision. Though she was sure he could take care of himself and Kelsey, she simply couldn't leave them unsupervised, she explained. She then implied that she wouldn't be allowed to keep them with her if anyone suspected she wasn't watching out for them at all times.

That point effectively ended the argument. The neighbor assured Ryan later that evening that Pip and Kelsey had been very well behaved.

As she tucked him in that night, Ryan thanked Pip for his cooperation. He gravely accepted her thanks and promised not to give her any further trouble about babysitters. Even though he didn't really need one, he seemed compelled to add in a murmur.

Ryan was smiling when she left the room.

Maybe this parenthood thing wasn't so hard, after all, she found herself thinking as she brushed her hair and prepared for bed.

MAX TOLD HIMSELF that the only reason he spent so much time with the kids during the next few days was because he felt sorry for them. Poor little orphans, now deprived even of the aunt who'd been appointed guardian to them.

Pip was obviously hungry for a man's attention. From what little he'd said of his aunt's boyfriend, the guy must have been a real jerk. He hadn't wanted to talk to the kids or have them interfere in his life in any way.

Ryan and the kids seemed to have worked out a comfortable routine. She fed them breakfast and drove them to school each morning. Her neighbor picked them up at school in the afternoons and took them back to the apartment, where she supervised them until Ryan got home.

Ryan left her shop now at seven most evenings, leaving her employees to close up. She was home to have dinner with the kids and spend time with them before tucking them in bed.

Max admired her dedication. He knew it wasn't easy for her to juggle work and the children's needs, but somehow she was doing it. Her employees seemed satisfied with the arrangement, the children were obviously thriving from her attention and business at the shop seemed steady whenever he was there.

He couldn't help worrying, however, that Ryan and the children were growing too close. Juliana had found her strongest lead yet on Essie Smith. She had already turned her information over to the authorities, and she expected the woman would be found before the week was over.

What would it do to Ryan, and to the children, when the woman came to collect her young relatives?

Wasn't that exactly why Max had always carefully avoided ties like this himself? Hadn't he seen years ago that getting too deeply involved with others always seemed to lead to heartache?

He hoped Ryan wouldn't be too badly hurt.

MAX WAS AT Ryan's apartment Thursday evening when she tucked the children into bed. He'd been around quite a bit during the past week, actually. She'd convinced herself that he'd come only out of concern for the children. He'd certainly made no further advances toward her.

Which, she assured herself each time the thought crossed her mind, was exactly the way she wanted it. Between work and the children, she had enough to occupy her time and her thoughts without having to deal with her befuddled feelings for Max Monroe.

"Coffee?" she asked him perfunctorily when they returned to the living room.

This was usually the point where he politely excused himself and made his exit. Tonight he hesitated only a moment before saying, "Yes, thanks. I'd like that."

Though she was a bit surprised by his acceptance, Ryan hid her reaction as she urged him to make himself comfortable while she went into the kitchen.

She could sense that he had something on his mind as he sipped his coffee. He appeared to be watching the evening news on television, but something told her he wasn't paying much attention to the headlines.

Finally, she set her own cup down and turned to him. "Is there something you want to talk to me about, Max?"

He made a rueful face and set his own cup next to hers on the coffee table. They sat side by side on the couch, some six inches separating them—physically. Ryan felt that they were even farther apart emotionally. She had no idea what he was thinking. She didn't even know why he was there.

"You're doing a good job with the kids," he said. "They look happy and healthy. Even Pip's starting to relax. He laughs more now, the way a kid his age should."

Ryan ran a hand through her hair. "I think they have been happier here than they ever were with Mrs. Culpepper. But they still worry about their future—especially Pip. He tries to hide it, but I can tell he worries about what's going to happen to them. That's why I haven't told him yet that his aunt is dead. Until I know more about what's to become of them, it would be cruel to leave him wondering."

"He never asks about her?"

"No," Ryan admitted. "He doesn't act as though he misses her at all. Neither of them do. Pip's greatest fear seems to be that he and Kelsey will be separated."

"Surely no one would separate them."

"Their aunts were planning to," Ryan reminded him.

"Yes. But that was when there were two aunts."

Ryan folded her hands in her lap. "If Essie wasn't willing to take both children before, I wonder how she'll feel about it now. Especially since she's apparently unemployed."

"We'll just have to wait and see."

"I know. But it's hard."

Max shifted on the couch, a slight frown creasing his brow. "Ryan...could we talk about something else for a while?"

She lifted a questioning eyebrow. "Like what?"

"Like...well, you."

"Me?"

Without smiling, he nodded.

"What about me?"

He brushed his knuckles against her cheek, the touch light, fleeting. It took her breath away.

"I'd like to know," he murmured, his face close to hers, "what you think when you look at me with those big, dark eyes. What you look like first thing in the morning, with your skin flushed with sleep and your hair all mussed around your face. I'd like to know what it is about me that makes you nervous. Sometimes you look at me like you're trying to figure out if I'm dangerous.

"But most of all," he added, sliding his hands into her hair, so that her face was cupped between his palms, "I'd like to know why I can't seem to get you out of my thoughts. Why I can't seem to stay away from you, even though I know I should. What is it about you that makes me think of you in the middle of the night when I can't sleep?"

She cleared her throat. "I think…"

His voice was a low growl. "What do you think?"

"I think you *are* dangerous," she admitted softly, helplessly. "At least to me."

His lips moved against hers. "You just might be right."

And then he was kissing her, taking her mouth in an assault that was no less devastating for being so very gentle. And she melted against him, just as she had before. Even though she'd promised herself it would never happen again.

Had it been his words that had shaken her defenses? His admission that he hadn't been able to stop thinking of her, just as she hadn't quite been able to put him out of her mind during the past few days, no matter how hard she'd tried?

Was it the way he looked, with his tumbled gold hair and his endearingly crooked smile, his devil-in-denim walk or his wicked, blue-gray eyes? His kindness to the children?

What *was* it about Max Monroe that made her want him, despite her absolute certainty that he could hurt her as no one ever had before?

She slid her arms around his neck, telling herself that she was going to stop this soon.

Just one more moment…

He pulled her closer, one arm around her, his other hand buried in the hair at the back of her head. His mouth teased, tasted, taunted, until she parted her lips and silently urged him to deepen the kiss.

Max promptly accepted the unspoken invitation.

Just one more moment, she thought, closing her eyes and losing herself in his arms.

"Ryan? Ryan?"

Kelsey's sleepy voice calling from the other room brought Ryan out of Max's arms with a gasp.

Disoriented, she pushed her hair away from her flushed face and stared at Max for a moment before turning on one heel to rush toward the children's room.

"Could I have a drink of water?" the little girl asked, rubbing her eyes when Ryan appeared in the doorway. "I'm thirsty."

Pip lifted his head from his pillow. "You should have asked me, Kelsey," he said groggily. "I'd have gotten it."

"Go back to sleep, Pip," Ryan said, relieved that her voice was reasonably steady. "I'll get the water."

She turned and almost walked into Max.

He steadied her with his hands on his shoulders. His eyes were dark and somber. "I'd better go," he said.

She nodded. "Maybe you should."

"We'll talk later."

She moistened her still-throbbing lips. "Yes."

"Good night, Ryan."

Her response came out as little more than a whisper. "Good night."

She didn't expect to sleep at all well that night.

10

CATHY CALLED RYAN to the telephone less than an hour after the shop opened Friday morning. "She didn't give her name," she explained. "She only said that she wanted to speak with you."

Thinking it might be Max's friend Juliana with some news for her, Ryan hurried to the phone. "Ryan Clark."

"Ms. Clark?" a husky voice at the other end of the line said tentatively. "My name is Essie Smith. I'm Peter and Kelsey's aunt. I heard you've been looking for me."

Ryan's fingers tightened convulsively around the telephone receiver.

"You're Essie Smith?" she repeated weakly, though she knew she'd heard correctly.

"Yes. I understand you've been taking care of my niece and nephew."

"How did you know?"

"The police contacted me this morning about…my sister. I called Mrs. Culpepper, and she gave me your number. She said she's been real sick and you've taken the kids in as a favor to her."

"I'm so very sorry about your sister, Ms. Smith. This must be a very difficult time for you."

Ryan thought she heard the woman draw an unsteady breath. "My sister and I weren't very close," she admitted after a moment. "But, yeah. It's hard."

"I'm sorry," Ryan repeated, not knowing what else to say.

"Look, I want to thank you for what you've done for the kids. Mrs. Culpepper said you were a friend of Opal's?"

Ryan moistened her lips. "Actually, I'm a friend of the children's."

"Oh. Well, I've made arrangements for Opal's things to be stored until I can get there. I've got a few things to take care of here and then I have to fly out to Utah to—to make arrangements for Opal. It's going to be a few days, maybe a week, before I can get to where you are. Will you be able to take care of the kids that long or do I need to figure out something else to do with them?"

Ryan frowned. Essie Smith had spoken so emotionlessly, as though the entire ordeal was a great nuisance to her. "Of course, I'll keep them with me," she said. "I'm very fond of the children. They're no trouble at all."

"That's good. At least I won't have to be worrying about them during the next few days. To be honest, I have enough to worry about."

"Ms. Smith," Ryan began hesitantly.

"Call me Essie."

"Essie, what *are* you planning to do with the children, if you don't mind my asking? Mrs. Culpepper told me that you and Opal had originally planned on splitting them between you—"

"That was Opal's idea," Essie interrupted. "She knew I didn't really want either of them. It isn't that I don't care about my brother's kids, but I'm really in no position to take care of them—especially both of them.

"To tell you the truth, Ms. Clark, I don't know what I'm going to do. I guess I'll just have to decide that when I get there. I'm sure there'll be a lot of legal matters to discuss with someone. I just don't know."

"Please, call me Ryan." Ryan felt a bit numb—a reaction to her surprise at actually hearing from this woman they'd been seeking for so long and to her renewed concern about

the children's future. "You have my home number if you
need me for any reason?"

"Yeah, Mrs. Culpepper gave it to me. Thanks. For everything, I mean. She says you're being real good to the kids."

Ryan was rather surprised by the landlady's praise. She
could only surmise that Mrs. Culpepper had wanted to jus-
tify letting her charges leave with someone who was in fact
a stranger to her.

"Please let me know when to expect you," she said as
they concluded the call.

"I will. Tell the kids—well, tell them hi for me," their
aunt finished lamely.

Ryan was genuinely depressed when she hung up the
phone.

Oddly enough, her first impulse was to call Max.

She dialed the number he'd given her in case she
needed him. He wasn't home. His recorded voice politely
requested that she leave a message if she wanted her call
returned. She hung up without speaking.

"What's wrong?" Cathy asked, studying Ryan's face.

Ryan explained. "She didn't sound overly concerned
about the children," she added when she'd summarized
the call. "She seemed more worried about how this would
inconvenience her."

"Sounds to me like she's thinking of giving them up,"
Cathy said, keeping an eye on the two customers brows-
ing through the merchandise.

Ryan bit her lip. "I thought so, too," she admitted.

"Well? Are you going to try to adopt them?"

Ryan tensed. "Me?"

"You aren't going to let them go to strangers, are you?
They're such sweet kids. What if they go to someone who
isn't good to them?"

Ryan twisted her hands. "You think I haven't considered that? I'm worried sick about them, Cathy. But—"

"So keep them. Nick's a lawyer. He can pull a few strings."

"But would that really be best for them? Pip and Kelsey need two parents, not a single mother with a full-time business to run."

"Lots of single mothers hold outside jobs," Cathy said with a shrug. "You've been managing this past week, haven't you? And this is your busiest time of the year, businesswise."

"Well, yes, but…"

"*Could* you support the kids?"

"I could probably swing it," Ryan conceded. "Money would be a bit tight, of course, but other single parents manage. I just don't know if it's the right thing to do. For any of us."

"It's something to think about, anyway," Cathy said. "Think about whether you really want to take on that commitment—and whether you can live with yourself if you don't."

Ryan winced. "That's a bit blunt."

"I know you, Ryan Clark. You aren't happy unless you're doing something for someone else. Those kids need you. And to be honest, I think you need them, too.

"And besides," Cathy added with a sudden, impish grin. "Who said you'd be a single parent for long, hmm? That gorgeous blonde who's been hanging around you so much the past couple of weeks isn't just interested in those kids."

Ryan was furious with herself for blushing. She was greatly relieved when one of the shoppers approached, carrying a number of fashion doll accessories.

But throughout the day Cathy's words echoed through Ryan's mind.

"ARE YOU SERIOUS about this, Ryan?" Nick asked later that evening, having unexpectedly dropped by her apartment just before the children's bedtime. He'd explained that he'd wanted to meet the kids, after hearing so much about them.

Ryan had noticed that both Pip and Kelsey reacted positively to her older brother, if not with the same enthusiasm they'd shown Max from the beginning. Now the children were in bed, and Nick and Ryan were talking over coffee in her kitchen. He wasn't smiling as he studied her across the table. "You're really thinking about trying to adopt these children?"

"I said it was something I was considering. I don't even know if it's possible. That's why I wanted to talk to you first."

Nick took a few minutes to think before answering. "It's possible, of course, assuming the aunt agrees," he said finally. "This state allows for privately arranged adoptions—I've handled a couple of them myself. But you'd have to be prepared, Ryan. It wouldn't be easy. The courts would still have to approve. And with you being young and single…"

"Other single people adopt children. Especially older children, like Pip and Kelsey. Most married couples want babies, isn't that right?"

"Usually," he agreed. "But I still don't want you to get your hopes up or to think that it's a snap to arrange. You should take a lot of time to think about this, Ryan."

"I'm not sure I have a lot of time," she said worriedly. "You didn't hear her, Nick. She said she didn't want the children—either of them. She never did."

"But do *you* want them? Really want them, I mean? When it comes down to it, you hardly know them. You met them—what? Two weeks ago?"

"Yes," she admitted, "but—"

"You're a single woman with a business to run and your whole life ahead of you, Ryan. Are you sure you're ready to sacrifice your freedom to raise two children who already have more than a few emotional scars? Are you sure you know what you'd be taking on? What you could be giving up?"

Ryan sighed. "I didn't say I thought it would be easy. But right now it doesn't seem such a sacrifice. You've met them. Can't you understand how hard it would be for me to just walk away from them?"

"Yeah," he agreed wryly. "Especially knowing you as well as I do."

"Everything really depends on Essie Smith," Ryan murmured, staring into her half-finished coffee. "And she won't be here for several days yet."

"That gives you more time to think about this."

She nodded. "But it wouldn't hurt for you to be looking into it in the meantime, would it? Just in case?"

"I'll look into it," he promised.

"And Nick—don't mention this conversation to anyone, okay? Not to Dad or Juliana or—or Max. I'm not ready to discuss it with anyone else yet."

Nick studied her face. "You don't think Max would be interested in hearing about this?"

"I'll tell him if—when I decide the time is right." She met his eyes squarely. "You won't say anything?"

"I won't say anything," he promised.

She relaxed—at least, a little. "Thank you."

BY LATE SATURDAY, Ryan was beginning to wonder if Max had left town without saying goodbye. Three times she'd tried to call him; the last time she'd even left a message on his machine. She hadn't heard from him since he'd kissed her and then left so abruptly Thursday evening.

Had Kelsey's unintentionally intrusive call for a glass of water made him realize how wrong he and Ryan were for each other? Did he suspect that she was becoming overly attached to the children, that she was ready for parenthood in a way that he was not? Had that scared him away?

If so, then good riddance to him, she told herself irritably. Hadn't she told herself all along that she didn't intend to get involved in an affair with him? If an affair was all he wanted, then fine. He could go.

So why did it hurt so much to think that she wouldn't see him again?

She'd been home less than an hour that evening when Max knocked on her door.

He looked tired, she thought when she first saw him. His dark blond hair was tousled, his eyes a bit shadowed. But his smile was as devastating as always.

"Hi," he said, his voice gruff.

She stood holding the door, torn between an impulse to walk into his arms and another to shut it in his face.

"Hi," was all she said in return.

"May I come in?"

She hesitated only long enough for him to notice, and then she stepped aside. "Of course."

"Max!" Kelsey ran straight into his arms, her little face glowing with pleasure. "Where've you been?" she demanded.

Holding her on his hip, her arms clasped around his neck, Max seemed to be studying Kelsey as he smiled at her. Ryan was aware of the differences he saw in the child from the first time he'd met her at the mall just two short weeks ago.

Kelsey was wearing one of the smart little outfits he had bought her, an oversize navy-and-red-plaid sweatshirt with red leggings and the new black shoes Ryan had picked up for her the other day. Ryan had carefully trimmed Kelsey's fine, white blond hair into a soft halo of curls, which she'd decorated that morning with a jaunty red bow. Kelsey looked healthy and happy, like an average six-year-old.

Pip stood nearby, waiting his turn to greet his idol. His sandy hair had been trimmed, too, though he'd rejected any trendy styles in favor of a conservative short cut. He wore a white sweatshirt with the picture of a popular television superhero printed on the front, new jeans and new sneakers. Ryan had made sure he'd had plenty of sleep during the past few days, as well as regular meals, and he, too, looked healthy and relaxed.

Anyone seeing him for the first time would see a normal, if rather quiet, nine-year-old boy, Ryan thought with a faint pang. Only those who knew him well—like her, and maybe Max—would see the faint shadows of insecurity at the back of his blue eyes. Pip was more keenly aware than Kelsey that their future still hung in the balance, that their present circumstances were only temporary.

Though Pip didn't speak of his concerns, Ryan couldn't help wondering how much time he spent worrying about the future. As much as she did, probably. The boy was like that.

Max finally got around to answering Kelsey's question about where he'd been. "I've been working, Kelsey," he explained, without looking at Ryan. "I'm on a deadline."

"What's a deadline?"

"I know what it is," Pip interrupted, eager to show off his knowledge. "It's a date when you have to have something done. Do you have a deadline for one of your books, Max?"

Pip had been terribly impressed to learn that not only was Max a published author, but—even more awe-inspiring—that there would be a movie made from one of his books.

Like many Americans, Ryan had thought wryly, Pip thought a truly good book was one that could be successfully adapted by Hollywood.

"Yeah, I've got a deadline," Max answered lightly, setting Kelsey on her feet. "I might even meet this one. Which would be a pleasant surprise for my editor."

"We were just about to order a pizza," Ryan told Max. "The kids wanted a special treat for Saturday dinner. Do you have a request for a topping?"

"Extra cheese," he said, still watching her a bit warily.

She nodded. "I'll call in the order. Pip, tell Max how well

you did on your history test yesterday. I'm sure he'll be very proud of you."

She went into the kitchen to use the phone, leaving Max trying to listen attentively as both Pip and Kelsey chattered to him at the same time.

Only when she was alone in the other room did she acknowledge to herself how very glad she was that Max had returned.

THEY SPENT THE EVENING eating pizza, playing board games and talking nonsense. The kids seemed to have a wonderful time.

Max and Ryan smiled and chatted easily enough, but Ryan was aware of the underlying tension between them, as she knew Max must be.

She let the children stay up a bit past their usual bedtime, but when she saw Kelsey yawn and rub her eyes, she knew it was time to call it an evening. She sent them off to wash up, brush their teeth and change into pj's, telling them they could take their baths in the morning.

At their request, Max helped Ryan tuck the children in. He settled them into their beds with smacking kisses and giggle-inducing tickles, then stepped aside to watch as Ryan smoothed the covers over them and kissed them good-night.

Kelsey came off the pillows unexpectedly as Ryan started to move away. Her little arms locked around Ryan's neck. "I love you," she said clearly, sweetly.

Ryan's heart quivered. She pressed her cheek into Kelsey's soft curls, holding the warm little body close to her own.

"I love you, too, sweetheart," she murmured huskily. "You *and* Pip."

Reluctantly, she loosened her arms and settled Kelsey back into the pillows. "Go to sleep now."

Max was watching her when she turned to leave the room. He motioned for her to precede him.

She turned back to face him when they were in the living room. "Now do you understand," she asked him quietly, "why I can't just give them up?"

"Yes," he said, and his eyes were grave. "I understand."

He didn't stay much longer. "Are you working tomorrow?" he asked as he prepared to leave.

"No, I'm taking tomorrow off to be with Kelsey and Pip. We thought we'd go to the children's museum and maybe out to a nice restaurant afterward."

"Do you mind if I join you?"

She was surprised, but she hid it. "I thought you had a deadline."

"Yeah. But I'd rather be with you. And the kids, of course," he added quickly.

She moistened her lips with the tip of her tongue and nodded. "Then I—we'd love to have you join us," she said.

He kissed her then—a slow, lingering, undemanding kiss that left her feeling warm and tingly, and aching for more. And then he was gone.

"YOU HAVE a very nice family, sir. Such well-behaved children. You must be very proud of them."

Murmuring a response, Max reacted with decidedly mixed emotions to the waiter's low-voiced words. It wasn't the first time that day that he and Ryan and the children had been accepted as a family. It had happened several times at the children's museum, and now at the end of a leisurely dinner in one of the area's premier Italian restaurants.

The children had been on their best behavior—polite and agreeable, eagerly open to new experiences. Ryan had made sure they looked nice—Kelsey in her red dress with the big white collar, white tights, black shoes, a red-and-green-plaid Christmas bow in her hair; Pip looking quite grown-up in a white shirt, a red sweater and navy slacks.

Ryan, of course, looked beautiful. She, too, had worn red—a long, figure-fitting dress of a soft, cashmerelike knit. Her dark hair was loose around her face. Cheery Christmasy jewelry sparkled from her ears, and the matching pin at her shoulder. Her hands were bare of rings, but that had apparently been overlooked by the strangers who'd assumed they were a family.

It occurred to Max that he'd like to have a photograph of the three of them, looking just as they did now. Like they belonged together.

If he tried really hard, he could almost imagine himself in the photograph with them.

Which, of course, scared him silly.

"Sir?" the waiter repeated, a bit louder this time. "Would you like to order dessert?"

"Oh, uh—yeah, sure," Max said, blinking and looking at the children. "You guys want dessert, don't you?"

"Ice cream," Kelsey said promptly.

"I'd like to see a dessert menu, please," Pip said, trying to sound sophisticated.

The waiter smiled. "Of course, sir."

Max allowed his thoughts to drift again as Pip and Ryan studied the menu and debated the relative merits of fruit-topped cheesecake or a sinful-sounding spumoni concoction.

He'd tried to stay away from this engaging trio. For almost forty-eight hours, after leaving Ryan Thursday evening, he'd paced his apartment, reminding himself that he wasn't interested in getting tied down. He wasn't the kind of guy who wanted commitments and obligations.

Did he really want to end up like his grandfather and his father—trapped in demanding, joyless relationships, sacrificing their freedom, their sense of adventure, their individuality to try to live up to society's expectations of sensible, responsible family men?

And then he remembered the way Ryan had felt in his arms. The taste of her. The deep-seated, undeniable *goodness* of her.

He'd never met anyone quite like her before. And he wasn't sure he ever would again.

And those kids…damn, but they got to him. Worried him. Made him wonder if some responsibilities would really be so bad, after all….

The dessert discussion seemed to have been settled. The waiter vanished, and Ryan and Pip sat back, anticipation in their satisfied smiles. Kelsey took a sip of her soft drink and then dabbed daintily at the corners of her mouth with her napkin, the way Ryan had taught her.

He'd really like to have a photograph, Max thought again. Just to look at when they weren't with him, to remember how much he'd enjoyed this day.

MAX HELD RYAN in his arms, his mouth hovering an inch above hers, his breathing ragged as a result of the kisses they'd already shared. The children had been in bed for almost an hour, and Max had been telling himself he'd go any minute now….

Just one more kiss, he'd promised himself.

That had been almost a dozen kisses ago.

"I really do have to go," he said with a groan, unable to tear his gaze away from her heavy-lidded eyes, her soft, kiss-darkened mouth.

"Yes," she whispered, though she seemed in no hurry to draw herself out of his arms.

He brushed his lips across the end of her nose. "It isn't easy to leave you," he murmured.

She looked up at him a bit shyly. "It's not?"

His mouth twisted ruefully. "No. What I really want to do is pick you up, carry you into your bedroom, lock the door and make love to you for days."

"I…" She stopped to inhale. Her cheeks darkened. "Oh."

He smiled, though he knew it was a strained effort. "Is that all you have to say? 'Oh'?"

"You have to know it sounds tempting to me," she said

quietly. "But under the present circumstances, it doesn't seem very likely."

"Because of the kids?"

"Partly," she agreed. "But mostly because of me. The way I am. What I need from a relationship. Even if the children weren't involved, I would have to have more than sex from any relationship. I'm not sure you're willing to offer more."

He sighed in resignation. "I was afraid you would feel that way about it."

"I always have, despite what happened between us before. This isn't something I take lightly, Max. I can't."

He ran a hand through his hair, putting a couple of inches distance between them. "You take *everything* very seriously, don't you?"

She took a deep breath, and he sensed that she was going to share something important with him. Something that would help him understand her.

"I told you I almost died in a car accident when I was almost eighteen," she began.

He nodded, remembering.

"My boyfriend was killed in that accident. We'd known each other since kindergarten and had been a couple for as long as I could remember. We were still just kids. We hadn't progressed beyond the kisses-in-the-dark stage of our relationship, but we were in love. I don't know if it would have lasted—I never had the chance to find out."

Max was startled. "You aren't still grieving?"

"No. Not the way you mean. But it still makes me sad when I think that Ricky died so young, so tragically. That he didn't live long enough to leave anything behind. Nothing but a few beautiful memories for the people who loved him.

"I made myself a promise then that my own miraculous survival wouldn't be wasted. I worked out a life plan for myself, and then I started following through with it. I wanted to travel, to make a little difference in the world, to own my own business. And I wanted a family. Someone to leave behind when it's my time to go, knowing I raised them with the same values and principles my parents instilled in me.

"I've accomplished quite a few of my goals," she continued, still boldly meeting his eyes. "In a relatively short time, I've done many of the things I dreamed of doing when I finished school. I still have quite a few career goals, a few more places I'd like to see and experience—but the most important dream of all hasn't yet come true. I was beginning to wonder if it ever would. Then Pip and Kelsey came into my life. And they need me. I can't help wondering if they're the family I was meant to have all along."

Max felt his chest tighten. He drew a deep breath, but it didn't help much.

He heard himself speaking almost before he knew what he was going to say. "When I was twenty-one, my best friend and I went off on an expedition to climb a mountain in Mexico. There was an accident on the way up. A rope snapped. My friend—Juliana's brother—was killed. I almost went with him."

"I take it you didn't come away from your near miss with the same lessons I learned," she said, her voice a bit husky with reaction to his stark words.

He shook his head. "I told myself I wasn't going to waste a minute of the time I had left. It looked to me like life was too short to get tied down with a lot of plans and goals that I might not even live to accomplish. Dan—my friend—had a lot of plans. A new career, a fiancée, dreams—all gone in the snap of a rope. My father had a lot of dreams, too. He gave them up for the path of respectability and responsibility. He died at fifty-eight of a massive heart attack, after forty boring, unfulfilling years."

"And what are *your* dreams, Max?" she asked quietly.

His mouth twisted. "I don't have any. But at least I'm still alive."

"Are you?" She stood without giving him a chance to answer. "You'd better go. It's getting late."

11

THAT NIGHT, Max couldn't stop thinking of that tragic time in Mexico, when he'd dangled from a broken rope on the side of a mountain, desperately scrambling for a foothold, knowing his friend was dead. He'd been scared then, more frightened than he'd ever been before or since.

Until now.

He felt the future looming ahead of him, as scary and uncertain as the abyss that had stretched beneath him on that mountain. Now, as then, he fought going into it, afraid of what awaited him if he let go of the present.

Could he walk away from Ryan and the kids?

Could he stay, taking a risk that he would never free himself if he did?

He could so easily picture Ryan with the children—making a life together. Planning a future for the three of them.

They would get along just fine without him, he was sure. But was that what he wanted?

He was aware of the loneliness of his silent apartment as he hadn't been in a long time. The loneliness of his life.

Oh, he could fill the emptiness. There were any number of women he could call who'd be happy to keep him company for a few hours. A few days. A few weeks. Until he tired of them, or they of him, at which point they'd part without regrets, without a backward glance.

He couldn't walk away so easily from Ryan. Something about her had already gotten a firm hold on him.

Was this love? The emotion he'd spent a lifetime avoiding?

If so, it was no wonder they called it "falling" in love. He found it every bit as frightening as being on the verge of falling off a mountain. He was beginning to wonder if it was every bit as permanent.

MAX KEPT HIMSELF scarce again during the week that followed. Ryan thought in exasperation that he was making her dizzy with this on-again, off-again behavior. Honestly, for a big, brave, macho sort of guy, Max Monroe was the biggest coward she'd ever met. Just talking about commitment made him turn pale and hide.

She still missed him.

The children came to the shop with her after school on Wednesday, since their baby-sitter was Christmas shopping that evening. Pip settled into the office with his homework, while Kelsey made a production of straightening the dolls on the shelves.

"I miss Annie," she said with a faint sigh as she came to the spot where the doll had once rested. A delicate Japanese doll was displayed there now, her almond eyes flirting over the top of a tiny, delicately painted fan.

Ryan had shown Kelsey at least two-dozen dark-haired, dark-eyed dolls during the past week. The child had politely admired all of them, but said that none of them was the same as her Annie. Ryan wished she knew what had been so special about that particular doll—which, she'd learned to her chagrin, was no longer in stock with the manufacturer. She still blamed herself for her carelessness in letting it get away.

Essie Smith called again on Thursday. Ryan answered the phone. She recognized the woman's voice with a sinking feeling. "When will you be here?" she asked.

"Probably on Saturday," the children's aunt replied glumly. "I've had a lot of things to take care of. Are the kids okay?"

"They're fine. We've been having a wonderful time."

"That's good. Have you, uh, told them about Opal?"

"No. I thought maybe you would want to do that."

"Lord, no!" Essie sounded disturbed by the very possibility. "I don't know them well enough to give them news like that. It would probably be better if you did it. Whenever you think the time is right."

Ryan massaged her temples. Maybe it *would* be better for her to tell them, she thought. But, oh, how she dreaded it!

"Have you—have you made any decisions about them?" she asked Essie tentatively. She was hesitant to discuss her own wishes over the telephone, but she needed to know if Essie Smith had been making arrangements for the children without her knowledge.

"No, not really. I've been thinking about it, though. If there was only one of them—the little girl, you know?—it wouldn't be so bad. A single woman like me could handle that. But a nine-year-old boy, now that's a different story. I don't know how I'll manage with both him and the girl."

"Pip's a very good little boy," Ryan felt compelled to say defensively. "He's no trouble at all."

Realizing that she wasn't exactly arguing in her own interests, she stopped and drew a deep breath. "We can talk about this more when you get here, okay? Call me when you arrive and I'll arrange to have you picked up at the airport."

"All right. Do you know any social workers around there I can talk to? Maybe someone who knows something about finding a foster family for the kids?"

"We'll find someone," Ryan promised, feeling a renewed surge of hope. If Essie was willing to place the children in a foster home, maybe she would be more receptive to Ryan's request to adopt them.

She intended to show the woman that she could provide a good home for the children, to demonstrate that they already loved her and she them. She could only hope Essie had enough familial feeling to want the children to go to someone who cared for them as deeply as Ryan did.

She couldn't help wondering if Max would be around when Essie Smith arrived.

MAX CALLED THAT EVENING, just after Ryan had put the children to bed. "How's it going?" he asked.

"Fine," she answered, wondering why the sound of his voice always turned her knees to jelly. "How's it going with you?"

"Fine. And the kids?"

"I just put them to bed. Kelsey has the sniffles. I hope she isn't coming down with something."

"Did you check her temperature? Have you called a doctor?" Max sounded genuinely concerned.

"She's not running a fever. And, no, I haven't called a doctor. It's only the sniffles, so far. Maybe that's all it will be."

"I bought her a gift today. A big stuffed bear that makes this weird giggle sound when you hug it. I thought she'd like it for Christmas."

Christmas, Ryan thought. Heavens, it was only ten days away! She hadn't done *any* shopping; she'd been too busy.

Would she still have the children with her when Christmas morning dawned? Oh, how she hoped to be with them then!

As though he'd read her thoughts, Max asked, "Has their aunt called?"

"Yes, she called this afternoon. She said she'll be here Saturday. I told her I'd have someone pick her up at the airport."

"I'll do it. Let me know what time."

Ryan hadn't really expected him to volunteer. She'd thought she'd ask Nick. "Are you sure?"

"Yeah. I want to talk to her."

"You won't say anything about my hopes to adopt them, will you?" She didn't want to sound ungracious, but neither did she want Max to confuse the issue with Essie Smith.

"Of course not. I'll let you handle that. I just want to see what she's like. Maybe I'll tell her what a great job you've done with the kids and how crazy they are about you."

"Just don't overdo it."

"I won't overdo it," he promised, sounding ruefully amused.

"Essie wants me to tell the children about Opal," she said. "I haven't done it yet. I didn't really know how to bring it up. When do you think I should tell them?"

"They're going to have to know soon," Max said after a moment. "Would you like me to be with you when you tell them?"

This new offer was the most surprising yet. Ryan would have expected Max to avoid a discussion of that gravity with a vengeance. "You wouldn't mind?"

"It's not going to be easy, is it?"

"No. It's not. And I'd appreciate your help. We can tell them tomorrow evening."

He assured her he would be there. "What else did Essie say about the kids?"

"Word for word?"

"Yeah. Word for word."

Ryan drew a deep breath, trying to remember. "Something like…if there was only one of them—Kelsey, preferably—it wouldn't be so bad. A single woman could handle raising a little girl alone. But a nine-year-old boy makes it different. It would be harder to manage taking care of both the kids alone."

"She wasn't talking about just giving Pip up for adoption, was she?" Max sounded appalled by the possibility. "Keeping Kelsey for herself?"

"I hope not," Ryan said grimly, having worried about

that prospect all afternoon. "If so, I'm going to have a very long, hard talk with her. I hope to change her mind."

"You'll have to make her see that it just isn't an option. Not with those two. But maybe it would be best to worry about that when the time comes. It won't do any good to get all steamed up about it now."

"No. I just want to be prepared."

He spoke briskly again, changing the subject without preface. "Tell me about your day."

She tried to follow his rapid change of mood. "What about it?"

"Everything. Sales figures, funny things that happened to you, weird customer stories…whatever you want to tell me. Let's talk about us for a change, shall we?"

Us. Ryan found it one of the most seductive words she'd ever heard. Even though she tried to tell herself it hadn't really meant anything.

STRICKEN, Pip stepped away from the living room doorway, holding his breath and tiptoeing so that Ryan wouldn't know he was there. He'd come out for a drink of water and had paused when he'd heard her voice.

He hadn't at all liked what he'd overheard.

"…If there was only one of them—Kelsey, preferably—it wouldn't be so bad," Ryan had said. "A single woman could handle raising a little girl alone. But a nine-year-old boy makes it different. It would be harder to manage taking care of both the kids alone."

Afraid that she would spot him, he'd backed away before she could say any more. He'd heard all he needed to hear.

Ryan didn't want him, he thought as he walked mechanically back to the bedroom he shared with Kelsey. She thought it would be too hard to raise two kids, especially him.

Just like his aunts, and like Aunt Opal's boyfriend, Ryan found him too difficult. Too stubborn, maybe, he thought sadly, remembering the displeasure he'd expressed when he'd found out she'd hired a baby-sitter to watch him and Kelsey in the afternoons.

He wished now that he'd kept his mouth shut.

He paused by Kelsey's bed, looking down at the innocent face illuminated in the soft glow of a night-light. She was sleeping soundly, her little mouth slightly parted, her ragged bear in her arms. So content.

Kelsey looked really pretty in the lacy white nightgown Ryan had bought her. It was trimmed with blue ribbons. Kelsey had said in awe that it was the most beautiful nightgown she'd ever seen. Ryan had laughed and hugged her and promised to buy her several more in different colors.

Pip understood why Ryan loved Kelsey. Who wouldn't? Kelsey was probably the prettiest, sweetest little girl in the whole world. That was why Pip had always wanted to take care of her, to make sure she had everything she needed and most of what she wanted.

Like parents.

He'd found Ryan for her, and Kelsey couldn't be happier. She'd told him just today that she hoped Aunt Opal would never come back, so they could stay with Ryan forever and ever. Pip had told her it wasn't very nice to talk about their aunt that way, but he'd secretly agreed.

He'd been happy here, too. Had been able to really relax for the first time since his mom and dad had died.

Now he had to leave. Kelsey didn't need him anymore.

He'd made the decision in the few short minutes it took him to walk from the living room to the bedroom. If he stayed, he would spoil Kelsey's chance of having a real home here with Ryan.

Maybe—Pip swallowed hard—maybe with Max, too. Max was nuts about Kelsey, of course. His eyes got all soft and warm every time she smiled at him.

Pip didn't know where he'd go, but that was okay. He could take care of himself.

Maybe he'd find a job. He'd been helping Ryan out a lot

at the store—unpacking boxes and sweeping the floor— whenever she'd let him. He had experience.

He swallowed and blinked back a film of tears. Leaving here was going to be hard. Really hard. But, for Kelsey, he would do it.

He leaned over and softly kissed his baby sister's cheek. "Be happy, Kelsey," he whispered. "Merry Christmas."

YAWNING, Ryan padded barefoot out of her bedroom, belting her terry robe at her waist. Her brain was taking a while to kick in this morning.

It was time to wake the children and get them ready for school—a typical morning in this new routine she'd suddenly found herself living. She smiled sleepily, quite content with the situation.

She noted at a glance that Pip's bed was empty. He must be in the bathroom, she thought, or already preparing his breakfast in the kitchen.

He was so accustomed to taking care of himself.

She touched Kelsey's shoulder. "Kelsey? Honey, it's time to get up."

Kelsey squirmed against her pillows, murmuring a sleepy protest.

Smiling, Ryan gave her a little shake. "Come on, sweetie, open your eyes. You have to get ready for school."

Kelsey sighed, opened her eyes, blinked a couple of times, then smiled. "'Morning."

Ryan leaned over to kiss a warm, sleep-flushed cheek. "Good morning. Did you sleep well?"

"Mmm-hmm. I dreamed about Christmas."

"Did you?"

"Santa Claus was there. The nice Santa Claus from the mall, not that grumpy one who rings the bell at the corner."

Ryan chuckled. "Sounds like a nice dream. Would you like to wear your black-and-green sweater with black jeans today?"

When Kelsey agreed, Ryan pulled the clothes out of a drawer and laid them at the foot of the bed. "I'll have your cereal ready when you're dressed."

"'Kay." Kelsey had already disappeared behind her soft white gown as she tugged it over her head.

Ryan noticed on her way to the kitchen that the bathroom door was open, the room empty. She pushed open the kitchen door, smiling brightly. "Good morning, Pip. You're up early…."

She paused, frowning curiously, when she noted that the kitchen, too, was unoccupied. There was no evidence that anyone had been in there that morning. "Pip?"

She retraced her steps—living room, bathroom, hallway, the children's room.

Kelsey was just snapping her jeans. She looked up in question. "I'm hurrying, Ryan."

"Have you seen Pip?"

Kelsey glanced automatically toward his empty bed. "No. Isn't he in the kitchen?"

"No." Ryan went into her own bedroom. No sign of him. "Pip?" she called, loudly enough to be heard anywhere in the apartment.

There was no answer.

She returned to the children's room. His bed was definitely empty. She even bent to look beneath it, and then, for some reason, in the closet. He wasn't anywhere to be found.

"Where in the world…?" Starting to panic now, she hurried back into the living room. The French doors leading to her tiny, fenced courtyard were locked, the courtyard empty. The front door was locked, too, but the dead bolt, the one that required a key, was unlatched.

Ryan opened the door and looked out into the hallway. She saw no one.

Closing the door, she pressed a hand to her forehead, trying to think what to do. A scrap of note paper on a lamp table caught her eye. She snatched it up.

She immediately recognized Pip's neat handwriting. *Please take good care of Kelsey. She loves you a lot.*

"Oh, God," she whispered, a sudden sick feeling radiating from the very depths of her. "Oh, Pip, *no.*"

MAX ARRIVED AT RYAN'S apartment less than fifteen minutes after her frantic call. He'd broken nearly every traffic law in the book getting there.

She threw the door open when he rang the bell. Her hair was tousled, she wore no makeup and she was hastily dressed in jeans and a sweatshirt. Her eyes were huge and shadowed. Distraught.

"I don't know why he left," she whispered against his chest when he took her in his arms. "Where could he have gone? What did I do wrong?"

"You've called the police?"

She nodded. "They're looking for him. I called Mrs. Culpepper. She hasn't seen him, but she's going to watch for him. Lynn and Cathy are going to open the shop today. If he shows up at the mall, they'll call us. Oh, Max, I don't know what else to do. Where could he be?"

Max gave her an encouraging hug, then set her a few inches back so he could see her face. "We'll find him, Ryan," he promised, trying to sound more confident than he felt. "We'll find him. Okay?"

She nodded. "I'm so frightened for him," she whispered.

"He'll be all right. Pip's good at taking care of himself."

Her eyes filled with tears. "He's just a little boy."

Max swallowed. "I know." It was all he'd thought of on the drive over—little Pip, wandering the streets alone.

Where *could* he have gone? And why?

A sniffle from behind him caught Max's attention. He turned to find Kelsey standing there, her ragged bear dangling from one hand, her face woebegone.

"Pip ran away, Max," she said, her voice quavering. "Why would he do that?"

Max picked her up and held her close. "We'll ask him when we find him," he assured her.

Someone knocked on the door. Once again Ryan rushed to open it. "Nick," she said, pulling her brother inside. "Oh, Nick."

Still holding Kelsey, Max watched as Nick hugged his sister. "How long has he been missing?" the lawyer asked, his voice urgent.

Ryan pulled away from him and began to pace. "It's been a little over an hour since I realized he was gone. I don't know when he left—sometime during the night, after I went to bed at around midnight. If anything has happened to him, I'll never forgive myself," she added in an anguished rush.

Kelsey shivered in response to the intensity of Ryan's tone. Max held her more closely. He met Ryan's eyes across the room and glanced meaningfully at the child in his arms.

He watched as Ryan made a visible effort to pull herself together. She drew a deep breath and pushed her hair away from her face. "All right," she said, her voice brisk now. "What should we do first?"

"Has anyone called Juliana?" Nick asked.

Ryan shook her head. "I didn't think of that."

"She's a P.I. She has some experience with this sort of thing. I'll give her a call."

"I'm going out looking for him," Max said, unable to simply sit and wait for word. "I have the phone in my car if you need to reach me, Ryan."

"I'll go with you," she said.

"Me, too," Kelsey volunteered instantly.

Max shook his head. "You two have to wait here," he said gently. "In case Pip calls, or anyone calls about him."

He could see the reluctance in Ryan's face as she nodded, conceding his point. He knew she'd rather be out searching for the boy—but where would she start? Max wasn't even sure where he was going to look. He just knew he had to do something. Pip's image haunted his mind, compelling him to action.

The thought of anything happening to the boy sent a sharp pain through Max's heart. He didn't like the helpless feeling that there might be nothing he could do to stop it.

He kissed Kelsey's cheek, then transferred her into Ryan's arms. He caught Ryan's chin in his hand, forced her to meet his eyes. "We'll find him, Ryan."

She studied his expression for a moment, seeming to find some reassurance there. "I'm sure we will," she said, trying to sound brave.

He kissed her roughly, quickly. "I'll stay in touch," he promised.

IT WAS THE LONGEST DAY of Ryan's life. The hours crawled past, empty and frightening.

Nick left soon after Max, saying that he was going to pick up Juliana and begin a search of their own. Every few minutes the phone rang—Lynn or Cathy, hoping for news; Max or Nick, reporting their depressingly unproductive steps; the police, asking for new details and suggestions.

By late afternoon, Pip still hadn't been found.

Ryan tried to keep up a brave front for Kelsey's sake. She assured the bewildered little girl that her brother would be found.

Kelsey couldn't understand why Pip had left her. Ryan had no answer for the child. Nor for herself.

All day she searched her mind for any clue as to why the boy would have felt compelled to leave. Had she done anything, said anything to upset him? Given him any reason to believe she didn't care about him?

Please take good care of Kelsey. She loves you a lot.

What had he meant? What had he been thinking?

Where had he gone?

It was almost 6:00 p.m. when Max returned. He looked tired. Defeated.

"Nothing," he said when she opened the door to let him in. "I've searched almost every inch of this town. There's no trace of him. Nick and Juliana are still out looking."

Ryan sagged against him. "Max," she whispered. "What are we going to do?"

His eyes were uncharacteristically flat, his voice raw. "I don't know."

Her lower lip quivering, Kelsey stood nearby, watching them with pleading eyes.

The telephone rang.

"I'll get it," Ryan said with a sigh, expecting it to be one of her friends again, asking for an update.

A man's voice responded to her cheerless greeting. "Ms. Clark?"

"Yes?"

"I understand you're missing someone."

Ryan straightened, her eyes narrowing. "Who is this? What do you know about Pip?"

She felt Max stiffen, then move closer to listen.

"Never mind who I am," the man said, his deep, pleasant voice sounding tantalizingly familiar. Ryan tried to place it, but couldn't.

"I think you should go to the park," he said. "Look around the football fields. You might want to hurry. It's dark and it's getting cold out."

"But who—"

"Goodbye, Ms. Clark. And Merry Christmas."

He hung up before she could ask anything more. The flat buzz of the dial tone sounded in her ear as she stood frozen, her fingers locked around the receiver.

"Ryan? Ryan, who was that? What is it?"

Max's urgent questions pulled her back into motion. She quickly hung up the phone and told him what the caller had said.

"He didn't identify himself? Didn't say how he knew about Pip's disappearance?"

"He sounded familiar, but…" Ryan stopped and shook her head. "I don't know who it was," she said. "But I have to go to the park."

"I'll go with you."

"But the phone—"

"Have your neighbor come handle it. She said she wants to do something to help. She can stay with Kelsey."

"No!" Kelsey's chin was set stubbornly. "I'm coming."

It was the first time Ryan had heard the child speak in quite that tone.

"Kelsey, maybe it would be better if you stay here," she said. "It's cold outside. We don't know that the man knew anything, really. It could be a waste of time."

"He's my brother and I'm coming! *Please*," she added, her eyes begging.

Max settled it. "Ryan, call your neighbor. Kelsey, get your coat. We should hurry."

12

THE PARK WAS NEARLY deserted—not surprising, considering it was after dark on a winter evening. It was a cloudy night, cold and damp. The moon struggled valiantly to cast some light through the thick layers of clouds overhead. Even the park lights seemed to be straining to provide sufficient illumination.

The few cars they passed seemed to be filled with teenagers cruising, maybe looking for a place to drink beer or make out.

A few cars made Ryan more nervous, as they held more-shady-looking adults. She didn't want to know why they were here. She didn't want to think about anything but Pip.

Was he here? Had she fallen for a sick, cruel attempt at a practical joke?

Max parked in the same spot Ryan had occupied the last time she'd come here looking for Pip. It was hard for her to believe it had only been three weeks ago. The children had become so much a part of her life during that short time that already she couldn't imagine living without them. Either of them.

Deep inside, she knew she felt the same way about Max. She simply didn't have time to stop and think about that now.

She threw open her door and jumped out. Kelsey followed her and took her hand.

Max had pulled a flashlight out of his car console. He aimed it toward the fields, which appeared to be empty.

"Come on," he said, motioning for them to follow him as he moved in that direction. "Let's look around."

"Pip?" Ryan called, hurrying after Max, with Kelsey trotting beside her. "Pip, are you here?"

"I thought I heard something," Max said, skidding to a halt on the damp, winter-dead grass. "Call him again."

"*Pip!*"

Max cocked his head, then broke into a run.

Catching Kelsey up in her arms, Ryan ran after him, hardly noticing the child's slight weight.

Pip had made himself a bed in a thick clump of bushes, obviously trying to stay warm. In the beam of the flashlight, his face was pale and frightened, his lips blue and quivering as he huddled in the lined denim jacket Ryan had bought for him.

Max had the boy in his arms before Ryan could reach them. "Pip," he said, his voice almost unrecognizable. "God, we were worried sick about you."

"I'm sorry," Pip said, burrowing into Max's arms. "I didn't know where else to go."

Kelsey squirmed to get out of Ryan's arms. Ryan set her on her feet. The six-year-old ran to her brother and patted his back, even as she scolded him. "Don't you *ever* do that again!" she told him fiercely. "You were a very bad boy to run away like that. Now you're grounded. For a month."

Ryan thought she would probably be amused that Kelsey had so firmly dispensed punishment—eventually. Right now it was all she could do to remain erect, the way her knees were shaking in relief.

She knelt beside Max and Pip, mindless of the dampness that penetrated her jeans. "Pip," she said, reaching out to touch him, needing to feel him. "Are you all right?"

Peering out from Max's chest, he nodded, his face wary. "I'm sorry if I worried you, Ryan. I didn't know you'd get so upset."

What had she done, she wondered again, to make him

believe she didn't care? How could she convince him otherwise?

"Pip, I love you. I was terrified that something bad had happened to you. If I've done something to hurt you or upset you, I'm very sorry. Can't we talk about it?"

"I—I heard you on the telephone last night," he said, pulling away from Max to face Ryan. "You said it would be easier for a single woman to raise one kid than two. You said if it was just Kelsey, it would be different. I wanted to make it easier for you. I wanted Kelsey to be able to stay with you. She loves you a lot," he added, repeating the words he'd written on that scrap of note paper.

Ryan was stunned. "Pip—sweetheart, you misunderstood. I wasn't talking about myself. I swear to you."

"She's right, Pip," Max affirmed. "She was talking to me last night, repeating something that—that someone else said. Trust me, they weren't Ryan's words."

Pip cocked his head, looking a bit suspicious. "They weren't?"

"Sounds to me like something Aunt Opal would have said," Kelsey commented, sounding much too mature for her years. "Or maybe Aunt Essie."

Pip turned back to Ryan. "I argued with you about the baby-sitter," he said miserably. "I shouldn't have done that."

Her eyes filled with tears. She blinked them back. "You had every right to express your opinion, even if I didn't agree. I was never angry with you for doing so. I love you, Pip. If I can, I want to keep you with me forever. Nothing you can do will ever change the way I feel about you."

She knew she'd been reckless in telling him that she wanted to keep him. She also knew she might be raising hopes she couldn't fulfill. But this child so desperately needed to feel loved. Wanted.

And Ryan was willing to fight with her last breath to keep him.

Somehow, she knew she couldn't lose. This battle would be fought for love. "Come home with me, Pip. Please."

He hesitated a moment longer, and then he threw himself into her arms. "I love you, too," he whispered.

And then he started to cry.

Holding him close, Ryan felt her own warm tears coursing down her cold cheeks. She wondered how long it had been since Pip had allowed himself to cry.

She would do everything in her power to make sure he never had cause to do so again, she vowed.

Max suddenly straightened, swung Kelsey up to his hip and held out his free hand to Ryan. "Let's go home," he said.

Holding Pip's shivering little form close to her side, Ryan took Max's hand. "Yes," she said, smiling at him through her tears. "Let's go home."

ESSIE SMITH ARRIVED the next day. A pale, haunted-looking woman in her late thirties, she carried herself with the weary stance of someone who almost expected disaster to befall her. Maybe, Ryan thought sympathetically, Essie had learned from bitter experience to expect the worst.

Sending Pip and Kelsey to Ryan's neighbor for a few hours, Max, Ryan and Nick spent the afternoon talking with Essie about the children. The woman, as well as grieving for the estranged sister she'd lost, was torn between her lingering loyalties to her dead brother's children and her concerns about her own future. She admitted frankly that she saw no way for her to provide the children with the care they would require.

It was then that Ryan made her request. "I would like to adopt them," she said, praying for courage. "I want to raise them as my own. I love them very much, Essie. I can give them a good home."

Essie studied Ryan's face. She didn't look surprised by the request. "You seem like a nice lady," she said after a while. "But you're still a stranger to me. I don't know what to do."

"It would be a privately arranged adoption," Nick said. "The terms can be pretty much anything you like, as long as they're agreeable to the courts. If you want visitation rights written in, we can do that."

Essie chewed her lip, obviously tempted. "You two aren't married?" she asked, including both Max and Ryan in the question.

"No," Ryan answered, feeling the warmth in her cheeks. "Max and I haven't really known each other very long. I would be the one adopting the children."

"You're sure about this?" Essie asked. "Absolutely sure? It won't be easy, you being single and all."

"I've never been more sure about anything," she replied, steadily meeting the woman's eyes. She could feel Max watching her, but she didn't look at him.

Essie sighed. "I watched the kids with you this afternoon. They're obviously crazy about you. And they're happy. Last time I saw them, they were real quiet and kind of sad looking. They don't look like that now."

Ryan thought of Pip's face when they'd found him in that park, alone and scared and unhappy. She hoped she'd convinced him in the hours since that he would never have to feel that way again.

She still didn't know who'd called her or how the man had known she was looking for Pip—but whoever he was, she was deeply, profoundly grateful to him.

"I will do everything in my power to give Pip and Kelsey a happy childhood," she promised.

Essie looked at Nick. "All right, Mr. Lawyer," she said, with a wry twist to her mouth. "I don't see as I really have any choice. I can't raise them, and I don't want to risk sending them to strangers who might not love them like your sister does. You draw up the paperwork. I'll sign whatever you need me to sign."

Ryan almost sagged in relief. Max's arm went around her shoulders. She welcomed his support, deciding not to try to analyze his actions just then. For now, she needed him and he was here. That was really all she could ask.

"It'll take several days to set the process in motion," Nick advised. "Probably be after the first of the year before everything's finalized."

"No hurry," Essie said with a shrug. "I got no immediate plans."

"Essie," Max said. "I'd like to help you out financially until you can find another job. Maybe I can make a few contacts for you. Would you allow me to do that?"

She looked at him narrowly, a woman who'd learned not to trust generous gestures from strangers. "Why would you do that? I already said Ryan can have the kids."

"It isn't a bribe," he assured her. "It's just an offer of assistance. You're the children's aunt, and you're having a run of bad luck. We're all sort of like family now. For their sake, and for yours, I'd like to give you a hand."

The woman lifted her chin proudly. "I'd pay you back. Once I'm on my feet again, of course."

"We can discuss that later," he offered.

She nodded. "Thank you."

The words sounded rusty. Ryan wondered how long it had been since she'd had reason to use them.

Max's arm tightened a bit around Ryan's shoulders, and for the first time she allowed herself to think about what had just taken place. The children were hers now. Once Nick had taken care of the legal details, no one could take them away from her.

Ryan began to smile, eager to face the challenges that lay ahead.

THE WEEK BEFORE Christmas was frantic. School let out for Christmas vacation, and the children split their time between the store, Ryan's neighbor and Max, who had them for several hours nearly every day.

Feeling rather guilty that she'd dumped so much responsibility on her employees during the past few weeks, Ryan spent long hours at her business, promising the children that things would slow down after Christmas—though not *too* much, she hoped, keeping her profits in mind. Business was encouragingly brisk, the sales exceeding Ryan's hopes.

She noticed in passing that there was a new Santa in the big rocker downstairs in the mall. She rather missed seeing the nice man with whom she'd shared an elevator. Someone told her he'd quit, having told everyone that he had a lot to do to get ready for Christmas. The mall employees thought it was quite a funny excuse.

The children had been told about their aunt Opal's death. They'd taken the news solemnly, thoughtfully.

Though both had expressed their regret, Ryan knew they would recover quickly. Opal hadn't encouraged them to love her and had given them no reason to become attached to her.

They were overjoyed that they were going to live with Ryan. Both Kelsey and Pip assured her that they couldn't have found a better mother if they'd picked her out personally. Ryan didn't quite understand why they both giggled when they said that.

They'd also made it clear that they wouldn't mind having Max become a permanent part of their new family. Ryan quickly changed the subject whenever their hints became a bit too pointed. Max didn't seem to notice. Ryan half expected him to take to his heels now that the children were settled in with her, but he kept coming back.

Essie joined them for dinner one evening. Still a quiet, somber woman, she actually relaxed enough to smile a few times during the meal.

She said she liked her new job at a men's clothing store

in the mall, as well as the apartment she'd leased in Mrs. Culpepper's building. She hoped to afford a better one eventually, but this was sufficient for now, she assured them. It was better than any other place she'd lived in a while.

Ryan hoped to convince Essie to remain a part of the children's lives. She firmly believed they needed that connection to their biological roots. She had always understood the importance of family.

Max had no plans for Christmas with his family, explaining that his mother was spending it in Hawaii with his sister's family. He said he would call them and that he had already sent gifts. He'd probably see them in the spring, he'd added with a shrug.

Ryan invited him to spend the holidays with her family. She and her brother always spent Christmas Eve with her father, she explained. They exchanged gifts and attended a candlelight church service together. This year she would be taking the children with her.

She would love it if Max would join them, she added a bit shyly. To her great surprise, he accepted.

It was a lovely evening. Ryan's father seemed delighted with Pip and Kelsey, and they were equally pleased with him. Ryan suspected that he would make a doting grandfather, just as Nick had already proved to be a devoted uncle.

Max's role in the family wasn't quite as clear. Ryan was aware of the questions in her family's eyes, but she made no effort to explain. How could she, when she didn't know herself exactly what Max had in mind for them?

RYAN WAS AWAKENED early Christmas morning by an eager shake of her shoulder. "Ryan, wake up," Kelsey whispered. "It's Christmas! Santa's been here. You should see all the packages he left under the tree! Oh, and Max is here," she added almost as an afterthought. "Are you getting up now?"

Ryan rubbed her eyes and peered at the clock. It was barely seven in the morning. Max was back *already?*

"I'll be right there," she said with a yawn. She and Max had stayed up very late the night before, making sure the packages were waiting to delight the children this morning. They'd both had a lot of fun playing Santa's helper for the first time.

Belting her white terry robe, she took the time to brush her hair and teeth and touch her dry lips with a bit of gloss, conscious of how she would look to Max. She would have liked to have showered, dressed and done her makeup before he saw her, but she knew the children's patience would never hold out that long.

She remembered Christmas mornings from her own childhood. She and Nick had hardly given their parents time to put on their slippers before dragging them into the living room to find out what Santa had brought.

Max was sitting cross-legged on the floor beside the Christmas tree he, Ryan and the children had decorated the week before. Kelsey sat in his lap, and there were piles of brightly colored packages surrounding them. He must have brought some of them with him this morning, Ryan realized. There were several she didn't recognize.

Pip greeted Ryan with a hug. "Merry Christmas."

She returned the embrace warmly, pleased that he'd felt comfortable making the first overture. "Merry Christmas to you, too, Pip."

Max looked up at her with a smile that sent a shiver down her spine. "Good morning."

"Good morning. Did you let yourself in?" She'd given him a key a few days earlier, telling him he might need it sometime for one of his outings with the children.

"Yes. Obviously, I just missed Santa. He'd already been here and gone."

"No one sees Santa when he's d'livering his presents, Max," Kelsey told him, as though he should already know that. "That's his magic."

"I thought it was worth a try," Max said with a shrug. "Doesn't he have to give me a pot of gold or something if I catch him?"

Kelsey dissolved into giggles. "That's not Santa. That's a lepper-con. You are so silly, Max."

He grinned. "A lepper-con, huh? My mistake."

"Anyone want breakfast?" Ryan asked, already suspecting the answer.

"Before we open presents?" Kelsey protested.

"I'm not really very hungry yet," Pip said, trying to sound offhand about it.

"Me, either," Max said. "Guess we could work up an appetite by tearing into some of these packages."

Ryan reached for the camera she'd left in a handy spot the night before. "Okay," she said with a smile. "Let's open presents."

The children didn't need to be urged twice.

Half an hour later the room looked as though a colorful tornado had blown through. Scraps of paper were everywhere, cheery bows peeking out of the wreckage. Toys were piled around the children, whose faces glowed with excitement. Ryan suspected they'd never had a Christmas quite like this one.

It was going to be difficult not to spoil them, she realized ruefully. They were so easy to please, having had so few privileges thus far in their short lives. She would have to take care not to overdo it.

Setting her own gifts aside, Ryan sat back contentedly and watched the others. Max and Pip were bent over a race-car set that Max seemed almost as excited about as the boy. Kelsey sat nearby, talking to the new doll she'd promptly dubbed Amelia.

Giving up the search for another Annie, Ryan had decided not to even try to choose one that resembled the dark-haired doll Kelsey had originally fallen in love with. She'd settled instead for a sweet-faced toddler doll with big blue eyes, long, curly red hair and a wardrobe of frilly little outfits. Kelsey had seemed delighted.

Ryan couldn't remember ever being happier.

"Now who's ready for breakfast?" she asked after a moment.

"I'm getting sort of hungry," Pip admitted.

"Me, too," Kelsey agreed.

"I could eat," Max drawled.

"Blueberry pancakes?" Ryan suggested. All three agreed with hunger in their eyes.

Smiling, she went into the kitchen to begin breakfast.

A moment later, she realized that someone had followed her. She looked over her shoulder to find Max standing close by, watching her.

He wasn't smiling.

"Did you come to help?" she asked, wondering at his somber expression.

He shook his head. "I came to give you your Christmas present."

She lifted an eyebrow. "But you already gave me a present. That lovely crystal box. It's a beautiful gift."

"I have something else. If you'll accept it." Taking a deep breath, Max held out a small, square package wrapped in gold paper.

Staring at it, Ryan swallowed. It was just about the size of a ring box, she thought, a flock of butterflies coming to life in her stomach. Had he…?

Her hand was shaking when she took it from him. She eyed him nervously before she opened it. He nodded.

It was, indeed, a ring box. The ring inside was stunningly exquisite, a large round diamond in a gold setting, accented with glittering baguettes.

Ryan felt as though the breath had just been knocked out of her. She could honestly say that this was the very last thing she had expected from Max. After all his warnings about not expecting commitments from him, he hadn't even hinted that he'd changed his mind. So when *had* he? And why?

"Maybe this isn't the right time—but it feels right," Max said, taking a step closer. "Will you marry me, Ryan?"

She clutched the ring box so tightly her knuckles ached. "Why?" she whispered, thinking of all the reasons she *didn't* want him to give.

If he was asking only for the sake of the children, because he felt obligated or thought they needed him, it would truly break her heart.

He gave her the only answer she would have accepted. "Because I love you," he said, his voice deep. Sincere.

She melted. It was all she could do to lift her chin and try one more time to be cautious. "You said you didn't want to be married," she reminded him. "You said marriage was a trap. That you wanted to be free."

"I've been doing a lot of thinking lately," he admitted. "I realized that I've been free for a long time. And I've been miserable. Maybe marriage *is* a trap, if you're married to the wrong person. But I'm beginning to see that with the right person, it's just the opposite."

"Are you so sure I'm the right person?" she asked in a whisper.

"Do you love me?" he asked in return.

"Yes." She answered without hesitation. She'd known she loved him ever since they'd made love together, though she'd been afraid to admit it, even to herself.

He smiled then, his eyes glowing. "Will you give me the freedom to be myself, even after we're married?"

"I wouldn't want you to be anyone other than who you are," she assured him huskily. "I would never try to change you or restrain you."

He took a step closer. "Will you let me be a part of your family? Will you help me raise our children—Pip and Kelsey and any we might have in the future—with love and laughter and a sense of adventure?"

"I can't think of a better way to raise children."

He touched her face. "Will you promise to love, honor and cherish, keeping only to each other—until death do us part?"

"I will." Her voice broke. She threw her arms around his neck. "Oh, Max, I will. I love you."

He crushed her to him and covered her mouth with his.

"Hey!" Pip said from the doorway several minutes later. "I thought we were having pancakes."

"Breakfast," Max said without releasing Ryan, "is going to be a few minutes late."

"That's okay. Take your time," Pip replied, a warm note of approval in his voice. "We'll have some of the candy from our stockings to hold us over."

He discreetly disappeared.

Max smiled and kissed Ryan again. She returned the embrace with fervent enthusiasm.

A moment later, she gasped and pulled herself out of his arms. "Candy?" she said. "Before breakfast? Pip!"

Max laughed joyously as she rushed to the doorway.

KELSEY DISAPPEARED later that afternoon.

Ryan and Max had been sipping hot chocolate in the kitchen, happily making plans for their future, having already called Nick to tell him their news and to let him know that they would both be listed on the adoption papers. The children, last they'd seen, had been playing with their new toys in the living room.

"Ryan? Have you seen Kelsey?" Pip asked from the doorway, looking a bit worried. "I can't find her anywhere."

The scare with Pip was still fresh in her mind, and Ryan shot to her feet. "Where have you looked?"

"All over the apartment. I can't find her."

Ryan and Max hurried into the living room. Kelsey's things were there, the new doll lying half-dressed on the floor, as though she had dropped it hurriedly.

Max dashed to the children's room while Pip checked

the bathroom. Both came back shaking their heads and looking worried.

"Kelsey?" Ryan called, wringing her hands. The new ring bit into her palm; she didn't even notice.

The patio door opened. Kelsey stepped inside, her face beaming. She looked surprised that everyone was standing there, watching her. "Ryan, look what I've got!" she cried.

Ryan hadn't even thought to look outside. She went limp with relief, chiding herself for overreacting. She noticed that Max, too, looked a bit sheepish.

"What..." She had to stop to clear her throat. "What were you doing outside, Kelsey?"

"Talking to Santa Claus. Look what he brought me!" The child was almost bouncing with excitement.

Puzzled, Ryan glanced down. Then froze. In Kelsey's hands was the dark-haired, dark-eyed doll from the shop.

"Kelsey," she said blankly. "Where did you get that?"

"It's Annie," Kelsey said, looking a bit impatient. "Santa brought her to me. She can be Amelia's big sister."

"He gave her to you just now?" Pip asked, looking in bewilderment from Kelsey to the French doors.

Kelsey nodded avidly. "He said he was sorry he was late, but he's been real busy. He gave me everything I asked for. Annie—and my new parents," she added with a sweet smile that included both Ryan and Max. "I told him it was my bestest Christmas *ever.*"

Ryan looked at Max, then both of them ran for the French doors. There was no one in the courtyard.

Peering over the privacy fence, Ryan thought she caught a glimpse of a man in red waving his arm to her. She blinked, but when she looked again, there was no one there. Mystified, she stared up at Max, who simply shrugged.

Pip and Kelsey were standing in the doorway, watching them. "He's gone," Kelsey said. "He said he was very tired and he needed to go rest now."

"I…" Ryan didn't quite know what to say. She looked again at the doll in Kelsey's arms.

Kelsey was still smiling, coyly now. "I already told him what I want next year," she said.

"What was that?" Max asked, a bit warily.

"A baby sister," she answered promptly. "He said he would see what he could do."

Ryan collapsed against Max's side as he choked and then laughed helplessly.

"You could have asked me first," Pip informed Kelsey heatedly. "*I* might have wanted a brother."

"Looks like we've got our work cut out for us," Max murmured, taking Ryan into his arms. "But something tells me we can handle it."

He kissed her then. Deciding to accept what she couldn't explain, Ryan kissed him back.

Neither of them noticed the sprig of mistletoe someone had hung on the doorway above their heads.

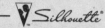

SPECIAL EDITION™

FROM *NEW YORK TIMES*
BESTSELLING AUTHOR

LINDA LAEL
MILLER

A STONE CREEK
CHRISTMAS

Veterinarian Olivia O'Ballivan finds the animals
in Stone Creek playing Cupid between her and
Tanner Quinn. Even Tanner's daughter, Sophie,
is eager to play matchmaker. With everyone
conspiring against them and the holiday season
fast approaching, Tanner and Olivia may just get
everything they want for Christmas after all!

*Available December 2008
wherever books are sold.*

Harlequin® Historical
Historical Romantic Adventure!

THE MISTLETOE WAGER
Christine Merrill

Harry Pennyngton, Earl of Anneslea,
is surprised when his estranged wife,
Helena, arrives home for Christmas.
Especially when she's intent on
divorce! A festive house party
is in full swing when the guests
are snowed in, and Harry and
Helena find they are together
under the mistletoe....

*Available December 2008
wherever books are sold.*

HH29525

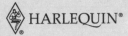
HARLEQUIN®

American ★ Romance®

HOLLY JACOBS
Once Upon a Christmas

Daniel McLean is thrilled to learn he
may be the father of Michelle Hamilton's
nephew. When Daniel starts to spend
time with Brandon and help her organize
Erie Elementary's big Christmas Fair, the
three discover a paternity test won't make
them a family, but the love they discover
just might....

**Available December 2008
wherever books are sold.**

LOVE, HOME & HAPPINESS

Inside ROMANCE

Stay up-to-date on all your romance reading news!

The Inside Romance newsletter is a FREE quarterly newsletter highlighting our upcoming series releases and promotions!

Click on the <u>Inside Romance</u> link on the front page of **www.eHarlequin.com** or e-mail us at insideromance@harlequin.ca to sign up to receive your FREE newsletter today!

You can also subscribe by writing us at: HARLEQUIN BOOKS Attention: Customer Service Department P.O. Box 9057, Buffalo, NY 14269-9057

Please allow 4-6 weeks for delivery of the first issue by mail.

IRNBPA208